THE VIRTUE OF VICE

SOMETIMES, WHAT WE LABEL AS VICE HOLDS THE SPARK OF UNIMAGINED VIRTUE.

AGAM AGRAWWAL

Made with ♥ on the Notion Press Platform
www.notionpress.com

Contents

Preface

Life unfolds as a canvas painted with hues of passion, challenge, and discovery. In the delicate interplay between clarity and mystery, I embrace both the logic of tradition and the allure of the unknown. With a mind steeped in creativity and a heart attuned to innovation, I navigate the ever-shifting tapestry of existence—unearthing hidden truths and reimagining the everyday into a vibrant narrative. Each moment is a verse in the grand symphony of life, inviting you to journey alongside as we blur the lines between reality and imagination, and uncover the profound beauty in every twist of fate.

Agam Agrawal

Prologue

In the twilight of an era defined by unwavering certainties, a subtle revolution began—a whisper rippled through society's fabric. In the interstices of conventional morality, it was here that the seeds of transformation took root. In a world once governed by the black-and-white edicts of virtue, the boundaries began to blur. What was once deemed sinful now shimmered with the promise of uncharted innovation, while the sanctity of tradition revealed its own hidden fractures.

Imagine a city where the luminescence of neon signs masks an undercurrent of defiance, where every alleyway hides stories of risk and rebellion. In this metropolis of inversion, the celebrated and the condemned find themselves intertwined, each breath stirring the pot of collective progress. The established order, built upon the pillars of conformity and control, trembles at the audacity of those who dare to transgress its sacred tenets. Here, the so-called vices are not the marks of moral decay but the sparks that ignite the engines of change.

In these shadows, the alchemy of contradiction unfolds—a realm where every act of defiance is a quiet act of creation. The risks once scorned by society now serve as the crucible in which new ideas are forged. A whisper of dissent can unravel a tapestry of old beliefs, weaving instead a fabric rich with possibility. Underneath the veneer of everyday life, there exists a dynamic interplay between darkness and light, where the unconventional becomes the catalyst for evolution.

As you journey through these pages, you will step into a narrative that challenges the very essence of right and wrong. The world you are about to enter is one where the rigid dichotomy of virtue and vice is dissolved, revealing a spectrum of human experience in all its messy, beautiful complexity. In this realm, the traits we have long dismissed as flaws are celebrated as the cornerstones of a new, transformative ethos—one that champions the courage to be different, the wisdom to embrace imperfection, and the resilience to redefine what it means to truly progress.

Welcome to the shadows of inversion, where every vice holds the potential for unimagined virtue, and every unconventional choice paves the way to a future yet to be written.

CHAPTER ONE

A World Turned Upside Down

The city of Luminex wears its polished façade like a cheap suit—a dazzling display of glass towers and digital billboards that pretends to champion modernity. But as the sun dips below the horizon and the neon lights flicker with a conspiratorial glint, Luminex reveals its true colors. Gone are the days when rigid moral codes dictated every breath; now, the old commandments are tossed aside with a mocking chuckle, replaced by a carnival of vice that the inhabitants celebrate as if it were the latest avant-garde trend. Who needs sanctimony when you can wallow in glorious, unbridled chaos?

Walking the slick, rain-slicked streets at night is like wandering through a twisted funhouse where every polished smile conceals a sardonic sneer. The citizens, once prisoners of conformity and mediocrity, now prance about in reckless abandon. In Luminex, risk isn't a stumble—it's the hottest currency, and every scandalous choice is paraded like a medal of honour. It's as if the city itself is grinning wryly, whispering, "Why settle for boring obedience when you can revel in delicious, debauched innovation?"

On a corner where a decrepit neon sign sputters its last gasps of colour, a battered café spills out the murmurs of disenchanted souls. Inside, the air is thick with bitter espresso and even more bitter humour. Mara—a former corporate drone who traded her tailored suit for a leather jacket and a voice that cuts through pretension—commands the room. With a sly twist of her lips and a dismissive flick of her wrist, she decries the old adage that risk is folly. “Risk,” she laughs, “is the heartbeat of progress.” Across from her, Theo, a young artist armed with nothing but his frayed notebook and razor-sharp wit, scrawls notes about the absurdity of a society that once cloaked its own decay in the guise of decorum.

The promise of the Carnival of Contradictions looms over Luminex like a mischievous specter. This isn’t your run-of-the-mill festival of frivolity; it’s a bold middle finger to outdated norms. Public squares will soon morph into arenas of subversive art and biting performances, where every act of defiance is cheered as a deliberate snub to conventional wisdom. Overnight, walls are adorned with murals that ooze ironic splendor—vivid, chaotic, and unapologetic displays that silently laugh at a past obsessed with order and control.

Deep in the underbelly of the city, in a long-abandoned warehouse reimagined as a den for the disillusioned, a motley band of intellectuals and misfits assembles. They’re not revolutionaries in the traditional sense; rather, they are connoisseurs of cynicism, savouring every crack in the edifice of outdated morality. Dr. Elias Marlow, once a revered sociologist now reduced to a bitter critic of moral pretence, stands at the centre. His voice, heavy with dark humour and a palpable disdain for the status quo, echoes off graffiti-stained walls. “For too long,” he spits out with derision, “we’ve clung to the delusion of decency. Now, every reckless act, every transgression, is our defiant shout into the void—a brilliant way of saying ‘enough’ to the absurdity of it all.”

His words, as sharp as broken glass, are met with a chorus of cynical nods and mumbled agreements. In that musty space, ideas ferment and bubble over into laughter—a laughter that is as much a weapon as it is a release. Here, the revolution isn’t about constructing a new utopia; it’s about gleefully mocking the ruins of the old world, laughing in the face of hypocrisy and celebrating every delightful misstep that defies convention.

Outside, as the night deepens, the city pulses with a raw, unfiltered energy. A street musician, his eyes closed in a manic reverie, strums a melancholic tune on a battered guitar, each chord a bitter reminder of life's beautiful tragedy. His music, a symphony of despair and defiant joy, underscores the notion that beauty can be found in even the most disordered moments. Meanwhile, in a modest apartment overlooking the chaos below, Lena—an insatiably curious writer with a penchant for unraveling society's pretence—stares out her window. The city's erratic glow fuels her thoughts, sparking a relentless barrage of ideas destined to peel back the layers of hypocrisy that have long veiled the truth of human existence.

As the night grudgingly gives way to a reluctant dawn, Luminex stands as a monument to shattered ideals. In this bizarre theatre of inverted values, every whispered act of defiance and every calculated risk is a piercing reminder: in a world that once glorified rigid order, true progress now arises from the darkness—the dark, sarcastic underbelly of our collective human folly. Here, the citizens have learned to dance on the wreckage of outdated conventions, embracing a truth that is as painful as it is liberating: that sometimes, the path to genuine innovation is paved not with noble intentions, but with the sharp, irreverent laughter of those who dare to question everything.

And so, as the first reluctant rays of sunlight creep over the horizon, Luminex awakens to a new, twisted reality. The city, ever defiant, stands poised on the brink of an era defined not by the constraints of moral righteousness, but by the raucous celebration of its most delicious contradictions. Every echo of rebellion, every sarcastic sneer at conformity, and every bold act of insubordination lays the foundation for a future where the established order is nothing more than a relic of a pretentious past. In this bold, unyielding vision, the very essence of progress is distilled into one irreverent truth: that sometimes, to create a better world, we must first laugh at the absurdity of the one we've left behind.

CHAPTER TWO

The Genesis of Vice

Before the neon rebellion took hold, Luminex was the kind of city that prided itself on a spotless reputation—a pristine monument to order where every citizen was expected to march in lockstep with the relentless beat of propriety. In this rigid environment, every rule was enforced with the zeal of a fanatic, each regulation a sacrament in the cult of conformity. The city's leaders, convinced of their own moral superiority, paraded their discipline like a badge of honour, blissfully unaware that every attempt to suppress the human spirit only served to stoke its hidden fires.

In those early days, the citizens of Luminex wore their civility like armour, convinced that decency was the ultimate shield against chaos. Yet beneath this polished veneer, the seeds of rebellion were already germinating. The more vehemently the powers-that-be denounced any deviation from their holy script of order, the more the people's hearts began to yearn for something raw, untamed, and delightfully forbidden. It was as if the very act of repression carried with it an ironic promise—a promise that what was condemned might, in fact, be the key to true liberation.

There were subtle signs at first—a furtive glance exchanged in a quiet corridor, a whispered joke laced with bitter irony in the dead of night. Intellectuals, artists, and even a few high-ranking officials began to question the absurdity of a society that worshipped rigidity while suffocating its own creativity. In hushed conversations in smoke-filled backrooms, these early dissidents would remark with dark humour how every prohibition served as an inadvertent invitation to explore what lay beyond the acceptable. “If you can’t have it, then by all means, make it the very thing that defines you,” one cynic quipped over a cup of tepid coffee, his voice dripping with sarcasm.

As the years wore on, the tension between enforced decorum and the natural impulse to rebel grew almost palpable. In the corridors of power, stern faces began to betray subtle cracks of doubt, while on the fringes of society, the allure of the forbidden blossomed. Behind closed doors, where the weight of societal expectations was lifted, people began to experiment with what they had long been told was sinful. What started as a secret indulgence soon turned into a full-blown subculture of defiance—a celebration of all that the old order had condemned.

In hidden enclaves scattered throughout the city, clandestine gatherings took shape. These were not your typical midnight meetings; they were riotous affairs where laughter was as common as the clinking of glasses, and every transgression was met with a knowing, conspiratorial smile. In one such meeting held in the crumbling basement of a derelict theatre, a group of renegade intellectuals and disillusioned bureaucrats convened to share their forbidden experiences. They spoke with a mix of bitter irony and gleeful rebellion, recounting how strict moral codes had only sharpened their desire to break free. Their conversations danced between philosophical musings and caustic jabs at the absurdity of a society that punished natural impulses with cold, unyielding discipline.

One of the most memorable voices in these gatherings was that of Vincent, a once-respected academic whose career had been stifled by his unwillingness to conform. With a sardonic glint in his eyes, Vincent would often remark, “Our society built these towering walls of decency only to imprison the very spark that makes us human. And now, as those walls crumble, we finally see that what they called vice was nothing but an echo of our deepest, most authentic desires.” His words, laden with dark humour and bitter truth, resonated deeply with everyone present, fuelling a slow but steady revolution of thought.

The contrast between the public and the private was becoming increasingly stark. In the polished corridors of government buildings and corporate boardrooms, officials maintained their stoic facades, their public speeches laden with platitudes about duty and honour. Yet behind those closed doors, many were indulging in secret escapades—rendezvous that defied the very standards they preached. Lavish affairs and clandestine trysts became the silent rebellion of the elite, a delicious irony that whispered, "Even we cannot escape the allure of the forbidden." These hidden indulgences were not driven by mere hedonism but by a deep-seated need to break free from the shackles of a prescribed existence.

Meanwhile, the cultural landscape of Luminex was undergoing its own quiet metamorphosis. Art, which had once been a tool for celebrating the sanitised triumphs of the state, began to shift its focus toward a darker, more subversive narrative. Paintings, once characterised by serene depictions of civic virtue, exploded with chaotic splashes of colour and raw, unapologetic emotion. Sculptures twisted into grotesque forms stood as stark reminders that beauty often lies in the imperfect and the forbidden. Poets penned verses that cut through the veneer of propriety with razor-sharp wit, their words an unflinching critique of a society that had lost its way in the pursuit of an unattainable ideal of perfection.

In music, too, the rebellious strain found its voice. Underground clubs, far from the mainstream venues sponsored by state-approved cultural bodies, became sanctuaries for those who dared to embrace the discordant symphony of their own lives. The pulsating beats and dissonant melodies of these secret gigs resonated with an audience eager to cast off the constraints of their overly regulated existence. Every chord, every lyric, served as a defiant shout against the sanitised narratives that had long dominated the public sphere.

The transformation was not instantaneous, nor was it universally embraced. There remained pockets of staunch traditionalists who clung to the old ways with a desperate, almost tragic tenacity. These guardians of morality, with their creaking moral compasses and sanctimonious proclamations, watched with a mix of disbelief and disdain as the very foundations of their society crumbled beneath the weight of its own hypocrisy. Their protests, both vocal and vehement, only served to highlight the absurdity of their position. In their eyes, every act of rebellion was a moral abomination; yet even they could not ignore the infectious energy of a culture that was rapidly evolving into something vibrant, if not entirely unorthodox.

One particularly illustrative moment came during a high-profile gala—a glittering event intended to showcase the finest examples of civic virtue. The elite gathered in a grand hall adorned with chandeliers and opulent decorations, each attendee meticulously groomed to embody the ideals of propriety. Yet as the evening unfolded, murmurs of discontent began to ripple through the crowd. It started with a single, sharply-timed remark—a toast that veered unexpectedly into dark satire, provoking stifled laughter and raised eyebrows. Soon, the carefully orchestrated façade of decorum began to crack. Conversations shifted from banal pleasantries to cutting critiques of the very standards they were supposed to uphold. What was meant to be a celebration of order slowly turned into an unspoken acknowledgment of the inherent chaos simmering beneath the surface. Even the most conservative among them found themselves momentarily captivated by the subversive allure of the forbidden—a fleeting glimpse of freedom in a gilded cage.

The genesis of vice in Luminex was, therefore, not the product of a single revolutionary act but the culmination of countless small rebellions—each one a deliberate, if subconscious, challenge to the stifling norms of a society gone mad with its own self-righteousness. Every prohibition, every whispered admonition to behave, had sown the seeds of its own undoing. The more the state tried to stamp out the natural impulses of its people, the more those impulses festered in the dark, growing into a potent force of rebellion that no edict could ever hope to contain.

As these subversive currents gained momentum, the fabric of Luminex began to change irreversibly. The city, once a pristine model of order, was gradually reimagined as a vast canvas on which the bold and the brash painted their visions of a more authentic existence. Every act of defiance, every indulgence in the forbidden, was a stroke in a grand masterpiece—a work of art that challenged the very notion of what was considered acceptable. It was a slow, almost imperceptible shift, a cultural mutation that transformed vice from a mark of moral failing into a symbol of creative liberation.

This transformation was as inevitable as it was ironic. For centuries, the citizens of Luminex had been taught to fear and abhor the darker aspects of their nature. Yet in repressing these elements, the state had unwittingly amplified their allure. The more society preached the virtues of discipline and restraint, the more the allure of passion, rebellion, and raw desire grew. In this paradox, vice became not only inevitable but also indispensable—a necessary counterweight to the stifling rigidity of imposed order.

By the time the undercurrents of rebellion had coalesced into a full-blown movement, the very idea of vice had been redefined. It was no longer seen as a moral failing but as a vital ingredient in the recipe for genuine progress. In the dim glow of underground gatherings, amid the clamour of subversive art and the raucous laughter of free spirits, the citizens of Luminex began to embrace a new philosophy. They celebrated the messy, unpredictable nature of human existence, recognising that in every act of defiance lay the potential for renewal and rebirth.

The irony was not lost on anyone. The architects of the old order, who had once preached the virtues of restraint and propriety, now found themselves unwitting participants in a grand, darkly humorous cosmic joke. Their carefully constructed rules had not stifled the human spirit—they had fanned its flames. And so, as the city of Luminex hurtled toward an uncertain future, it carried with it a legacy of defiance, a testament to the power of vice to transform and transcend even the most rigid of social orders.

In the end, the genesis of vice in Luminex was a story of evolution through contradiction—a saga in which every attempt to suppress the inherent wildness of humanity only served to unleash it in ever more audacious forms. It was a tale as old as time, yet told with a bitter, knowing wink; a narrative where the darkness was not a flaw to be eradicated, but a feature to be celebrated. And in this celebration lay the promise of a new world—one in which the beauty of the forbidden was no longer hidden in the shadows but stood boldly in the light, challenging every notion of what it meant to be truly alive.

CHAPTER THREE

Flawed Heroes and the Beauty of Imperfection

In the bitter haze of a sleepless night, when Luminex's neon glow had long since surrendered to the oppressive weight of darkness, our misfit heroes gathered once more in the abandoned heart of an old warehouse district. This was not a place of sanctuary in the conventional sense—it was a battleground for those brave enough to claim the beauty of their own flawed existence. Here, every shattered window and graffiti-stained wall bore witness to the riotous parade of human imperfection, and every echo in the empty corridors mocked the sanitised ideals of the world above.

Mara arrived first, her silhouette cutting through the gloom like a wry joke whispered at midnight. No longer confined by the rigid expectations of a life spent in sterile boardrooms, she now revealed in her chaotic freedom. With a sardonic twist of her lips and a deliberate swagger in her step, Mara moved through the derelict streets as if they were a runway for the unapologetically damned. In her eyes burned the bitter, defiant glow of someone who had tasted the venom of perfection—and spat it out with relish. Every scar on her face and every wrinkle etched into her expression was a testament to battles fought against a society that once demanded she be immaculate. "I've learned," she often mused under her breath as she passed darkened alleys, "that the more you try to erase your flaws, the more they stain you like ink on paper." Tonight, like every night, her arrival heralded the promise of yet another chapter in the endless, absurd play of rebellion.

Theo joined her not long after, his presence as quiet and enigmatic as a half-forgotten poem. Clutching his battered notebook—his constant companion and the repository of his deepest, rawest truths—he drifted alongside Mara. His face, gaunt and illuminated by the intermittent flicker of streetlamp, bore the melancholic weariness of a man who had seen too much and yet, paradoxically, still believed that beauty was hidden in the very wreckage of life. "Only the broken can see," he would often say with a weary smile, "that every crack in the façade is an invitation to discover something real." His words were not preachy; they were a resigned confession—a dark humour arising from the acceptance that the pristine veneer of society was nothing but a lie.

The duo made their way toward The Crucible—a former textile mill that had been transformed into a rebel's den by those who refused to be swallowed by conformity. The building loomed like a dilapidated monument to forgotten dreams, its rusted metal and crumbling brickwork serving as the perfect backdrop for a gathering of souls who wore their scars with pride. Here, the misfits and outcasts converged to share their tales of triumph through failure, to laugh at the absurdity of a world that celebrated perfection while quietly mocking every honest flaw.

Inside, the air was thick with the acrid scent of burnt coffee and stale cigarettes—a pungent reminder that here, in this forsaken enclave, the pursuit of perfection was replaced by the raw immediacy of lived experience. A motley assortment of characters filled the space: Cassian, whose once-glossy political career had been reduced to bitter anecdotes; Silas, the enigmatic wanderer whose quiet observations cut deeper than any sword; and Elara, a tender soul whose gentle voice belied a fierce determination to redefine beauty on her own terms.

Cassian, seated at a scarred wooden table in a far corner, regaled a small group of rapt listeners with tales of his past glories and subsequent downfalls. "I once believed," he began, his voice rough with a lifetime of regret, "that integrity was the highest virtue.

But integrity, as I learned the hard way, is just another word for hypocrisy when it's forced upon you. We built these magnificent towers of decency only to watch them crumble under the weight of our own pretensions." His words, steeped in bitter irony, resonated deeply with the crowd. Even as he mocked the very idea of virtue, there was an unspoken acknowledgment that his own failures were the only honest proof of his humanity.

Silas, leaning casually against a chipped brick wall near the centre of the room, interjected with a soft chuckle. "You see," he said in his measured, almost melodic tone, "in every scar lies a story. In every failure, a lesson. Our flaws—they're not imperfections to be hidden, but the very brushstrokes of an authentic masterpiece. If perfection were attainable, we'd all be sterile, soulless replicas of a myth." His words, though delivered with quiet conviction, were laced with the kind of cynical humour that only a man who had traversed the darkest corners of human desire could muster. "In our brokenness," he added, "we find the truth. And in truth, there is an almost exquisite freedom."

Elara, who had been silently observing from a shadowed corner, finally spoke up, her voice soft yet unwavering. "Every wound, every bruise," she whispered, "tells us that we are alive. And in the scars that mark us, there is a beauty that no glossy facade can ever replicate. We are living, breathing testaments to the chaos of existence." Her eyes, shimmering with unshed tears and a fierce inner light, scanned the room. In that brief moment, it was as if every person present felt the weight of her words—a collective acknowledgment that the very things they had once considered shameful were now their greatest assets.

As the evening unfolded, the conversation in The Crucible grew more animated. The rebels debated fiercely, their voices rising in a cacophony of bitter satire and passionate defiance. They questioned the validity of a world that demanded conformity while ignoring the inevitable decay at its core. In one heated discussion, a young poet named Rafe challenged the notion that failure was something to be celebrated. "What do you expect?" he scoffed, slamming his fist on the table, "Our society has been built on the bones of the fallen. It's a monument to the failure of our collective arrogance. We are nothing more than the byproducts of a system that worships an unattainable ideal." His words, though harsh, carried an undercurrent of resignation—a recognition that the very structure they were fighting against was so deeply ingrained that it defied simple reform.

Mara, ever the provocateur, smiled wryly at Rafe's outburst. "Oh, Rafe," she said, her tone dripping with sarcastic affection, "you forget that it is precisely because we have been beaten down by the relentless pursuit of perfection that we now find beauty in our flaws. Our failures are the stepping stones to something far more genuine than the sterile dreams of our oppressors." The room fell silent for a moment as her words sank in. In that silence, each person reflected on the irony of a society that had tried so desperately to erase its own imperfections—only to create a void that now teemed with the raw, unfiltered truth of human existence.

Outside, the rain continued to fall, a relentless cascade that transformed the slick streets of Luminex into mirrors of fractured light and broken dreams. The city itself was a living metaphor for the rebellion unfolding within The Crucible. Its towering skyscrapers, symbols of corporate ambition and artificial perfection, glistened in the distance like wounded sentinels. Yet in the narrow, forgotten alleyways, life thrived in unexpected, messy bursts—graffiti that defied the sterile blankness of corporate walls, street performers whose raw passion brought colour to an otherwise grey existence, and whispered confessions of love and loss that echoed in the dark. It was in these hidden corners that the true spirit of Luminex lived—a spirit that refused to be contained by the empty promises of progress.

As the night deepened, the rebels of The Crucible began to disperse into smaller, more intimate clusters. In one such secluded nook, Mara and Theo found themselves alone, their conversation a private exchange of bitter truths and half-forgotten dreams. "You know," Mara confided, her voice dropping to a conspiratorial whisper, "there was a time when I believed that perfection was something to aspire to. But the more I tried to mould myself into that image, the more I realised it was nothing but a prison—a gilded cage that suffocated every spark of rebellion." Theo listened intently, his eyes reflecting a mixture of empathy and weary resolve. "I've always thought," he replied, "that our scars are the only honest maps of our lives. They tell us where we've been, what we've endured, and perhaps even hint at where we're meant to go." His words, simple yet profound, were a reminder that even in the midst of relentless despair, there existed a glimmer of hope—a hope that true beauty could only be forged in the crucible of imperfection.

Their exchange was interrupted by the arrival of a figure who seemed to materialise from the very shadows—a woman known only as Verity. Clad in a tattered coat and with eyes that burned like molten lead, Verity exuded an air of mystery that commanded attention. "We are all fragments," she declared, her voice resonating with an almost hypnotic cadence, "fragments of a larger, broken whole. Each of us is a piece of a puzzle that the world refuses to see. But in our fragmentation lies our strength, for together we form a mosaic of truths that is far more powerful than any singular, polished lie." Her words, delivered with a mix of conviction and quiet fury, struck a chord with everyone present. In that moment, the assembled rebels realised that their individual battles—fought in the darkness of their own despair—were part of a larger war against the tyranny of a perfection-obsessed society.

In the hours that followed, the discussions turned toward action—a plan, not of violent upheaval, but of cultural revolution. The rebels, fuelled by their shared disdain for a world that had long exiled imperfection, began to craft a manifesto. This document, to be disseminated in clandestine pamphlets and scrawled in digital corners of the internet, would articulate their vision: a world that embraced the raw, unfiltered truth of human existence, where every flaw was not a mark of failure but a badge of honour. They envisioned art shows in abandoned warehouses, poetry readings in forgotten basements, and street murals that would challenge the sterile, homogenised narratives of corporate propaganda. It was an audacious plan—a subtle insurgency designed to awaken the slumbering masses to the beauty of their own imperfect souls.

For the next several days, The Crucible became a hive of frenetic activity. Mara, with her unwavering determination, coordinated meetings with underground artists, musicians, and even a few renegade intellectuals from the upper echelons of society. Cassian, ever the cynic, served as a reluctant advisor, his dark humour a constant reminder of the absurdity of the status quo. Silas and Verity took charge of the creative communications, crafting messages that were as biting as they were beautiful—a blend of dark satire and passionate idealism that would soon find its way onto the walls of Luminex in the form of subversive street art.

In one memorable gathering, held in the dim light of a derelict factory, a heated debate erupted over the very nature of authenticity. "What is authenticity?" demanded a young woman named Nia, her voice trembling with indignation. "Is it merely the act of baring one's soul in the face of relentless judgment, or is it something more—something that transcends the petty labels we've been forced to wear?" The room fell silent as her question hung in the air, heavy with the weight of unspoken truths. After a long moment, Cassian spoke up, his tone both scornful and reflective. "Authenticity," he declared, "is the realisation that every attempt to appear perfect is nothing but a cruel lie. We are authentic when we embrace our contradictions, when we allow our scars to tell the story of who we truly are." His words, rough and uncompromising, resonated with everyone present. In that moment, it was as if the very idea of perfection—so relentlessly pursued by the world outside—crumbled into dust, leaving behind only the raw, unadorned truth of existence.

As the manifesto took shape, the rebels began to consider how best to disseminate their message. Underground zines were printed in small batches, their pages filled with bitter poetry, candid confessions, and satirical critiques of the modern obsession with flawlessness. Digital channels, too, became battlegrounds for ideas, as carefully edited images and unfiltered videos circulated among those hungry for something real—a stark contrast to the glossy, sanitised narratives peddled by mainstream media. Every piece of art, every carefully chosen word, was an act of defiance—a way to reclaim the narrative from a society that had long prized conformity over chaos.

In the midst of this creative fervour, Theo found himself retreating to a secluded corner of an abandoned park on the outskirts of Luminex—a place where nature, in its own rugged way, had reclaimed the scars of urban decay. There, among the rusted remnants of forgotten machinery and the overgrown tendrils of resilient weeds, he sought solace in solitude. With his notebook in hand and the sound of the wind whispering through broken trees, Theo began to write with an urgency that was both cathartic and transformative. His words flowed like a river of raw emotion, capturing the essence of a generation that had long rejected the sterile ideals of perfection in favour of a truth that was as messy as it was beautiful.

He wrote of love and loss, of triumph and tragedy—the timeless interplay of light and shadow that defined the human condition. In his verses, the pain of rejection was interwoven with the bittersweet joy of defiance; the agony of broken dreams was tempered by the fierce determination to rise again. Every line was an ode to the irreverent spirit of those who had chosen to live on their own terms, even if it meant bearing the scars of a world that had never truly embraced them. "We are the shards of a once-whole mirror," he penned, "scattered by the relentless pursuit of an unattainable ideal. But in our fragmentation, we discover a beauty that is raw, unfiltered, and utterly ours."

Back at The Crucible, the manifesto was completed by the early hours of a rain-washed morning. The rebels gathered one final time to read aloud the document that would serve as their collective battle cry—a declaration that authenticity, in all its flawed splendour, was worth more than the sterile promises of perfection.

As each person took a turn reading their chosen lines, the room filled with an almost tangible electricity—a sense that, for the first time in a long while, their voices were not being stifled by the oppressive weight of expectation. Their words, laced with sarcasm and dark humour, cut through the haze of despair like a beacon, signalling the dawn of a new era.

And so, with the manifesto in hand, the rebels of Luminex stepped out into the emerging light of a new day. They carried with them the raw, unvarnished truth of their collective experience—a truth that celebrated every flaw, every failure, every delicious imperfection that made them who they were. The streets, still slick with rain and alive with the echoes of their nocturnal defiance, became the canvas for their message. In the form of bold murals and subversive graffiti, their manifesto was emblazoned on the walls of the city—a constant reminder that the pursuit of authenticity was an act of rebellion in itself.

In the days that followed, as whispers of their movement spread through the alleys and underground channels of Luminex, a subtle transformation began to take root. The sterile gloss of corporate propaganda was gradually overlaid with the gritty textures of real life—a collage of images that celebrated the raw, unpredictable beauty of imperfection. Even in the high-rise offices and manicured parks of the city, people began to question the relentless pursuit of an unattainable ideal. Conversations that had once been confined to the dim recesses of The Crucible spilled out into the daylight, challenging the established narratives with a bitter, knowing humour.

Mara, Theo, Cassian, Silas, Verity, Elara, Nia, Rafe, and countless others became the vanguard of a cultural renaissance—a movement that did not seek to destroy the old order outright, but to transform it from within. Their actions, though subtle, set in motion a ripple effect that gradually eroded the rigid structures of a society that had long rejected its own imperfections. Every time a passerby paused to read a subversive mural or a clandestine zine, the seeds of rebellion were sown anew. And though the forces of conformity fought tooth and nail to maintain their stranglehold on power, the truth of the rebels' manifesto proved an unstoppable tide—a tide that promised a future where every scar was celebrated and every flaw honoured as a testament to the unyielding human spirit.

In the end, the movement was not measured by grand, sweeping gestures or violent upheaval; it was measured in the small, everyday acts of defiance—a sarcastic remark shared in a crowded elevator, a secret smile exchanged between strangers on a rain-soaked sidewalk, a whispered acknowledgment that, in a world obsessed with perfection, the real beauty lay in being unapologetically, irreverently human. And as Luminex continued its relentless march toward an uncertain future, its neon heart beating with a rhythm of defiance and dark humour, the flawed heroes pressed on—each step, each breath, a quiet, persistent rebellion against a society that had forgotten how to celebrate the exquisite poetry of imperfection.

Thus, in the sprawling, chaotic tapestry of Luminex, where every shattered dream and every bitter laugh told a story of triumph over sterile conformity, the revolution of authenticity continued unabated. For in the realm of the imperfect, every misstep was not a failure but a bold stroke in a masterpiece that only the brave could ever hope to create. And as the sun climbed higher in a sky streaked with the muted hues of a hard-won dawn, the rebels of The Crucible vowed to carry their message forward—one sarcastic, defiant, and beautifully flawed moment at a time.

In the relentless interplay of shadow and light, where despair and hope intertwined in a bitter, ironic dance, the truth remained undeniable: perfection was a lie, and the only genuine beauty lay in the scars of those who dared to live unfiltered. For Mara, Theo, and their band of renegades, every day was a testament to the raw power of imperfection—a promise that even as the world crumbled under the weight of its own sanitised ideals, the spirit of authentic rebellion would forever burn bright in the hearts of the beautifully broken.

And so, as Luminex stirred awake to another day of conflicted promises and fractured dreams, the legacy of that dark, unforgettable night endured—a legacy of sarcastic defiance, of bitter revelations, and of a hope so fierce it could only be born from the very depths of imperfection. For it was in the acknowledgment of their own flawed humanity that the rebels found the courage to challenge the established order, to rewrite the narrative with every defiant breath, and to prove once and for all that in a world starved for authenticity, the raw, unpolished truth was the most revolutionary force of all.

CHAPTER FOUR

Embracing the Dark: The Allure of Risk

Risk was not merely an abstract concept in Luminex—it was the currency of life, the elixir of revolution, and the bitter delight of those who dared to defy the neat, sterile boundaries of a society obsessed with perfection. In this decaying city of neon and irony, the allure of risk pulsed through every darkened alley and under every flickering streetlamp. It was an invitation to abandon the safety of mediocrity and plunge headlong into the unknown, where every dangerous turn held the promise of a truth that was as raw as it was unsettling.

On a night when the rain fell in relentless sheets and the city's glistening surfaces reflected a million fragmented images of its own decay, Mara set out on one of her most daring escapades. She had long learned that the safest path was the most dangerous of all, for safety meant surrendering to the relentless, soul-crushing weight of conformity. Instead, she craved the thrill of uncertainty, the delicious terror of stepping off the precipice into a void where the rules no longer applied. Tonight, she planned to scale the side of a glass tower—a symbol of the corporate dystopia that had once dictated every aspect of her life—and plant a banner that mocked the sanitised dogma of the elite. With every sinew coiled like a spring, she moved silently through the labyrinth of backstreets, each step an act of defiance against a society that had taught its citizens to fear the unknown.

As she approached the monolithic structure, Mara paused in the shadow of an old, graffiti-laden wall. The dark reflections in the puddles at her feet were a constant reminder that beauty was often hidden in the decay of abandoned dreams. "Risk is our only salvation," she murmured with a wry smile, her voice carrying a hint of bitter irony. "It's only by dancing with danger that we learn what it truly means to be alive." With that, she pressed her back against the cold surface of the building and began her climb—a precarious ballet on the edge of oblivion. Every grip, every movement was calculated yet instinctive, a blend of practiced skill and raw, unfiltered audacity. As she ascended, the city below sprawled out like a chaotic mosaic of light and shadow, a reminder that in Luminex, even the highest towers were built upon a foundation of fragility.

Halfway to the summit, as the wind whipped around her like the whispers of discontent, Mara couldn't help but laugh—a short, dark chuckle that bordered on manic. "I suppose there's no greater thrill than defying gravity and common sense at the same time," she thought. It was in these moments—when risk and danger coalesced into an intoxicating cocktail—that the truth of existence revealed itself. The higher she climbed, the more the artificial order of the city below disintegrated into a swirling vortex of possibility. Each precarious handhold was a small rebellion, every shift of her weight an act of repudiation against the calculated perfection of a society that prized safety above all else.

At the summit, Mara paused to catch her breath, her heart pounding a rapid, defiant rhythm that seemed to echo the city's restless pulse. In the distance, the sprawling urban landscape stretched out like a vast, imperfect canvas—a living testament to the interplay of chaos and order, of beauty emerging from ruin. With a deft flick of her wrist, she unfurled the banner. The fabric, dark and tattered at its edges, bore an inscription in jagged, hand-painted letters: "Embrace the Dark. Risk is Life." It was a statement that resonated with the misfits and rebels who prowled the underbelly of Luminex—a challenge to the suffocating dogma of safety and conformity.

Down below, unbeknownst to the polished suits and complacent souls of the corporate world, a small group of dissenters had gathered to witness Mara's latest act of subversive artistry. In a forgotten park, nestled between the sterile modernity of glass and steel, they huddled together beneath a flickering streetlamp, their eyes reflecting a mixture of awe, defiance, and unspoken understanding. Theo was among them, his notebook clutched tightly as if it were the only tangible proof that truth could still be written in the margins of society. His gaze was fixed on the towering structure above, where Mara's silhouette danced against the night sky like a living embodiment of rebellion. "That's the allure of risk," he whispered to a nearby friend, his voice low and reverent. "It's the only spark that can ignite the fire of change in a world gone cold with certainty."

The spectacle of Mara's audacity was but one chapter in a larger narrative—a narrative that spanned the lives of many in Luminex, where risk was woven into the fabric of everyday existence. In the dark corners of the city, behind closed doors and beneath the veneer of normalcy, individuals embraced the allure of danger in myriad ways. There were those who defied the system by trading secrets in hushed tones over cheap whiskey, whose whispered confessions carried the weight of lives spent at the edge of chaos. There were others who found solace in the thrill of illicit affairs, where every stolen moment was a rebellion against a society that sought to confine them within narrow definitions of propriety. And then there were the artists, the poets, the musicians—all of whom saw in risk not a Spector of impending doom, but a muse that spurred them to create beauty from the wreckage of a sanitised world.

One such artist was Cassian, a once-prominent political figure whose career had been derailed by the very hypocrisy he had once championed. Now, stripped of the pretence that had once cloaked him in respectability, he roamed the streets as a living testament to the intoxicating power of risk. Cassian's fall from grace was not a tragedy in the conventional sense—it was a metamorphosis, a bitter yet liberating rebirth that taught him to value the unpredictable nature of life over the rigid, suffocating promise of safety. "Risk," he would say with a sardonic smile as he sipped from a dented flask in a rundown dive bar, "is the only currency that matters. You can spend all your money and build walls around yourself, but walls are meant to crumble. Only when you live on the edge do you truly learn what it means to be free."

His words resonated with those who had long since rejected the sanitised narratives of success. In the dim light of the bar, where cigarette smoke curled like spectral fingers around patrons' faces, Cassian recounted the tale of the time he had risked everything on a single, audacious gamble—a moment when he had stood before a room full of dignitaries and declared that their promises were nothing but empty platitudes. "I looked them in the eye," he recalled, his voice a gravelly echo of defiance, "and told them that the only thing worth risking was the chance to be real. And if that cost me everything, then let it cost me dearly." His confession was met with raucous applause and bitter laughter—a shared acknowledgment that, in embracing risk, one might lose it all, yet gain something infinitely more valuable: the unvarnished truth of existence.

For many in Luminex, risk was not a calculated venture into the abyss, but an art form—a dance with destiny where every misstep was as illuminating as it was dangerous. In the neon-lit backstreets and under the indifferent gaze of towering skyscrapers, risk became a way of reclaiming the self—a means of stripping away the layers of pretence that society had imposed like a suffocating shroud. There was a particular thrill in the act of stepping into the void, of daring to exist in a realm where failure was not only possible, but inevitable. It was this inevitability that lent risk its seductive charm, a reminder that the path to authenticity was paved with the wreckage of shattered illusions.

Theo, ever the introspective poet, found himself captivated by the paradoxical allure of risk. In the solitude of his cramped apartment, where the walls were lined with scraps of paper bearing the fragments of his thoughts, he would often reflect on the delicate balance between fear and desire. "The greatest risk," he would scribble in his notebook during sleepless nights, "is not the danger that lurks in the shadows, but the suffocating comfort of a life lived without daring." His verses were imbued with a longing for a freedom that lay beyond the safe confines of predictability—a freedom that could only be attained by embracing the dark uncertainty that lurked at the edge of every decision.

It was not uncommon for Theo to wander the rain-soaked streets at dawn, seeking inspiration in the interplay of light and shadow. One particularly overcast morning, as the first tentative rays of sunlight struggled to pierce the heavy gloom, he found himself in a deserted square. The silence was profound—a stark contrast to the cacophony of rebellion that reigned in the night. Yet in that silence, he discovered a beauty that was both haunting and exhilarating. The empty expanse of the square, with its cracked pavement and forlorn lampposts, became a canvas for his thoughts. "Risk is the heartbeat of life," he murmured to himself, "a relentless reminder that every moment is a chance to defy the ordinary." And as he walked on, each step resonated with the quiet conviction that only those who dared to confront the darkness could ever hope to see the true light.

Meanwhile, back at The Crucible, the rebels continued their nocturnal revelry with an intensity that bordered on the frenzied. The air was alive with the clamour of impassioned debates and the clinking of mismatched glasses—a chaotic symphony of voices united in their shared contempt for a world that had long prized safety over truth. In one corner, a group of radical thinkers discussed the idea that risk was not an act of madness but an essential ingredient for evolution. "Without risk," one of them declared, his eyes glinting with fervour, "we would be nothing more than automatons—soulless beings trapped in a cycle of predictable monotony." His words, delivered with a blend of biting sarcasm and fervent idealism, ignited a spark of agreement that soon spread like wildfire through the room.

Among those who listened was a woman named Livia, whose presence was as enigmatic as it was captivating. With a voice that was both husky and resonant, she recounted her own journey—a path marked by audacious risks that had led her from the depths of despair to the exhilarating heights of liberation. "I was once paralysed by fear," she confessed, her tone soft yet resolute, "afraid to step beyond the boundaries of what was expected. But then I realised that true freedom lies in the willingness to risk everything—to embrace the possibility of failure and in doing so, to uncover the hidden treasures of our own potential." Her story, told in a series of halting yet impassioned sentences, resonated deeply with those who had gathered around her, each person finding in her words the courage to confront their own fears.

As the night wore on and the boundaries between revelry and introspection blurred, the notion of risk took on an almost mythic quality. It became the thread that wove together the disparate lives of those who dared to live on the fringes—a thread that connected the daring exploits of Mara with the introspective musings of Theo, the bitter recollections of Cassian with the fervent declarations of Livia. In every whispered conversation, in every defiant act that defied the carefully curated narratives of the establishment, risk emerged as both a challenge and a promise—a promise that the future belonged to those who were willing to venture into the dark unknown.

At one point, as thunder rumbled in the distance and the storm outside reached a fevered pitch, Mara found herself engaged in a heated debate with a newcomer—a young idealist named Julian whose eyes shone with the untested fire of youthful audacity. "Risk is reckless abandon," Julian argued, his voice trembling with the zeal of conviction, "a fool's errand that leaves you vulnerable to the whims of fate." Mara's laugh was low and sardonic, a sound that seemed to carry the weight of all the disillusioned souls who had ever dared to defy the status quo. "Ah, Julian," she replied, her tone dripping with cynical amusement, "reckless abandon may be a fool's errand, but it is also the only route to authenticity. The moment you choose safety over risk, you resign yourself to a life devoid of truth. And trust me, truth is far more dangerous—and infinitely more exhilarating—than any carefully constructed illusion."

Their debate, punctuated by the howling wind and the rhythmic patter of rain on metal, encapsulated the essence of what risk meant in Luminex. It was a visceral, unyielding force that compelled individuals to confront the very core of their being—to acknowledge that the only way to achieve greatness was to flirt with the possibility of total collapse. In the eyes of those who lived by this creed, every dangerous leap, every heart-stopping moment of uncertainty, was not an act of foolishness but a bold declaration of independence from a world that valued conformity above all else.

Over the course of the long, storm-laden night, the rebels of The Crucible shared stories of moments when risk had altered the course of their lives. There were tales of forbidden romances that blossomed in the shadows, of business ventures that teetered on the edge of ruin only to soar to unexpected heights, of personal sacrifices made in defiance of a system that rewarded mediocrity. Each story was a testament to the paradox of risk—that the very act of embracing danger, of stepping into the unknown, could transform despair into hope and failure into a stepping stone toward something greater.

Julian, listening intently to the cascade of testimonies, began to see the beauty in the chaos. His youthful idealism, once tinged with the fear of the unknown, was slowly being replaced by a fierce, albeit raw, understanding of what it meant to truly live. "I've spent so long clinging to the idea of security," he admitted in a quiet moment, his eyes scanning the faces of those around him as if seeking validation, "that I forgot that life's greatest moments are born from risk. It's the dark, unpredictable path that leads to the brightest lights of realisation."

In that moment, a palpable shift occurred—a collective recognition that risk, with all its inherent dangers, was the crucible in which the human spirit was forged. The conversation turned to the inevitability of failure, not as a mark of defeat but as a necessary companion on the road to authenticity. "Every failure," Cassian said with a gravelly chuckle, "is a badge of honour. It tells you that you dared to dream, that you risked the very essence of your being in the pursuit of something real." His words, laced with a bitter wisdom, resonated deeply with the gathered rebels, each person silently acknowledging that the scars of failure were far more meaningful than the empty accolades of a society that celebrated only the flawless.

As dawn approached and the storm's fury subsided into a melancholic drizzle, the rebels of The Crucible gathered their scattered thoughts. The night had been long, fraught with confessions and revelations, with debates that had oscillated between biting sarcasm and raw vulnerability. Yet amid the cacophony of voices, one truth emerged unchallenged: the allure of risk was not merely about defying the odds—it was about reclaiming the right to be imperfect, to be unapologetically alive in a world that demanded sterile perfection.

Mara, standing at the threshold of the now-quiet building, surveyed the rain-washed streets with a gaze that was both resolute and reflective. "We are all addicted to risk," she murmured to herself, the words a soft incantation against the dying embers of the night. "It's the dark spark that sets us free—a reminder that to truly live, we must be willing to lose everything, to embrace the uncertainty, and to celebrate the chaos that is our existence." In that moment, as the first pale hints of dawn broke through the lingering gloom, she understood that the risk was not just an act of rebellion—it was a way of being, an eternal dance with the unpredictable forces of life.

Theo, leaning against a graffiti-smeared wall as he scribbled the final lines of a new poem, felt that same stirring of possibility. The ink flowed from his pen with a fervour that spoke of battles fought in the quiet recesses of the soul—battles where the stakes were nothing less than the very essence of one's identity. "To risk is to live," he wrote, "to plunge into the abyss with eyes wide open, knowing that every moment may be your last, yet revealing in the glory of the unknown." His words, etched onto paper with an urgency borne of both pain and passion, were a rallying cry for all who had ever dared to defy the suffocating certainty of a measured life.

In the days that followed, as the echoes of that stormy night reverberated through the dark corridors of Luminex, the movement born of risk began to seep into every corner of the city. Graffiti that bore the words "Risk is Life" appeared on brick walls and corporate billboards alike, a subversive reminder that the pursuit of perfection was a trap from which no one could escape. Underground art shows flourished in abandoned warehouses, their exhibits a riotous celebration of the imperfect, the dangerous, and the gloriously unpredictable. Digital platforms, too, became battlegrounds for ideas, as anonymous posts and viral videos challenged the sanitised narratives of mainstream media with the raw, unfiltered truth of lived experience.

Everywhere, the allure of risk ignited a quiet revolution. It was evident in the furtive glances exchanged by lovers in the shadows of overpass bridges, in the bold defiance of a street performer who danced atop a speeding bus, in the whispered confessions of those who had risked everything for a taste of forbidden freedom. In Luminex, risk was no longer a word spoken in hushed tones or relegated to the margins—it had become the lifeblood of a generation that refused to be tamed by the iron grip of conformity.

As months passed and the seeds of rebellion took root, the legacy of that fateful, storm-swept night continued to grow. The manifesto of authenticity, scrawled in dark ink and bitter truths, was disseminated through every available channel. It became the rallying cry of a movement that saw beauty in every fall, every misstep, every moment of audacious vulnerability. And with each new act of defiance, the citizens of Luminex began to understand that the true power of risk lay not in the absence of safety, but in the courage to embrace the inherent chaos of life.

Thus, in the relentless cadence of rain and neon, in the silent symphony of shattered dreams and wild aspirations, risk emerged as both muse and mentor—a teacher that schooled the disenchanted in the art of truly living. It was the dark, seductive whisper that promised liberation to those who dared to listen; it was the roar of the tempest that washed away the tired illusions of certainty, leaving behind the raw, pulsing heartbeat of a world reborn in its own beautifully broken image.

And so, as Luminex continued to pulse with the defiant energy of its imperfect denizens, the allure of risk became an enduring anthem—a declaration that the only way to transcend the cold, mechanical predictability of a sterile existence was to surrender oneself fully to the glorious uncertainty of the unknown. In that surrender lay the paradoxical truth: that in risking everything, one might finally discover the priceless reward of a life unbound, a spirit unchained, and a soul forever illuminated by the fierce, unyielding light of authentic rebellion.

CHAPTER FIVE

The Catalyst of Change: When Vice Ignites Innovation

The city of Luminex had long been a living contradiction—a place where sterile facades of corporate perfection masked the raw, unbridled chaos simmering beneath. In this unforgiving urban theatre, vice had slowly morphed from a whispered sin into a full-throated rallying cry. It wasn't merely about indulgence; it was the spark that ignited transformation. For those who had been cast aside by the draconian rules of order, vice had become the catalyst of change—a fuel for innovation that burned brighter than any sanctioned idea.

On an overcast afternoon that promised rain and a taste of urban decay, a series of clandestine gatherings began to ripple through the underbelly of Luminex. In smoky backrooms and forgotten warehouses, renegades and eccentrics huddled together, fuelled by a shared conviction that the old paradigms were not only broken but fundamentally corrupt. Their mantra was simple: only through embracing what society had long condemned could they shatter the chains of mediocrity and herald a new era of creative revolution.

In one such gathering—a dimly lit basement tucked beneath the skeleton of an abandoned factory—a motley crew of innovators, artists, and disillusioned former insiders gathered around a battered metal table. Their faces were marked by the passage of time and the weariness of battles fought against a system that prized conformity over authenticity. Among them was Dr. Alistair Kane, a disgraced former engineer whose once-promising career had been derailed by his refusal to adhere to conventional methods. Alistair's eyes, dark and intense, scanned the room as he began to speak in a measured, sardonic tone.

"Let's be perfectly clear," he said, his voice echoing off the cold concrete walls, "the so-called innovators of our time have been nothing more than glorified bureaucrats. They cling to outdated models and sanitised formulas that kill creativity. But we—by daring to flirt with vice, by embracing the raw edges of our humanity—are the ones who will disrupt this charade." His words, laced with bitter irony, resonated deeply with the assembled group. They knew that every act of rebellion, every seemingly reckless decision, was a deliberate strike against the sterile boundaries that had once dictated every aspect of life in Luminex.

Across the room, Marisol—a brilliant yet unconventional technologist with a penchant for turning chaos into code—nodded in agreement. "Innovation isn't born in boardrooms full of safe bets and polished speeches," she interjected, her tone dryly amused. "It's forged in the fires of risk. Every time we choose the unpredictable, every time we flirt with the forbidden, we send shockwaves through the system. We force the old guard to reckon with the fact that their safe, controlled world is nothing but a gilded cage." The room erupted in murmurs of approval, and for a moment, it felt as if the weight of a century of bureaucratic oppression was beginning to lift, replaced by the palpable thrill of imminent revolution.

As the meeting progressed, the conversation shifted from abstract ideals to concrete examples. Alistair recounted how a group of renegade engineers had bypassed the strict protocols of their corporate overlords by developing an unorthodox energy solution—one that harnessed the chaotic power of urban waste and converted it into sustainable power. "They risked everything," he said, "and in doing so, turned what was once seen as a vice—waste, decay, the byproduct of a failing system—into a beacon of innovation. That's the true irony: the very elements society scorns are the raw materials for genuine progress."

Marisol then presented her latest project, a daring piece of experimental software designed to disrupt the conventional order of data. With a few deft keystrokes on her battered laptop, she demonstrated how her algorithm could predict market fluctuations by analysing the "noise" that most analysts discarded as irrelevant. "The data that flows from the margins—the chaotic, unfiltered information that the elites call 'garbage'—contains patterns, insights even," she explained. "If we learn to read that noise, we can forecast trends before the so-called experts even know what hit them. That's innovation born of chaos." Her presentation, punctuated by wry laughter and knowing nods, was a testament to the idea that the vices of randomness and disorder were not weaknesses, but potent forces waiting to be harnessed.

Outside, the rain began to fall in heavy sheets, drenching the neon-lit streets and transforming the cityscape into a glistening mosaic of reflection and distortion. It was as if nature itself had decided to join the chorus of rebellion—a reminder that even the elements were in on the secret: that the predictable was overrated, and that there was beauty in the unexpected.

Back in the basement, the conversation turned to the impact of these innovations on the fabric of Luminex itself. A younger member of the group, Javier—a street artist whose murals had become underground icons—spoke passionately about the transformative power of vice-driven creativity. "Every time I spray a wall with a piece that challenges the sanitised narratives of the elite, I'm not just making art—I'm making a statement," he declared. "I'm saying that our mistakes, our flaws, our very human missteps are what make us vibrant. The system wants us to be perfect, but it's our imperfections that spark true change." His voice, raw and unfiltered, cut through the haze of cigarette smoke and skepticism, inspiring even the most jaded among them.

In that moment, as the basement filled with the cacophony of defiant voices and visionary ideas, it became clear that vice had transcended its traditional role as a mere indulgence. It had become a catalyst for innovation—a transformative force that, by embracing the dark, unpredictable aspects of life, could reshape the very foundation of society. The rebels of Luminex, united in their commitment to live authentically and defy the established order, understood that their path was fraught with risk. Yet it was precisely that risk—the willingness to venture into the unknown, to challenge the status quo—that held the promise of a future where creativity and progress were not stifled by fear.

As the meeting wound down and the rebels began to disperse into the stormy night, the basement was left buzzing with residual energy. The manifesto of their shared vision—one that celebrated the unconventional, that turned vice into virtue, and that saw chaos as the birthplace of new ideas—was still unfolding in every whispered conversation, every shared laugh, every resolute nod. Outside, the streets of Luminex continued to pulse with the defiant rhythm of rain and neon, a cityscape that bore silent witness to the quiet revolution taking shape beneath its glittering surface.

Mara stepped out into the deluge, her thoughts a swirling mix of adrenaline and anticipation. The act of scaling that glass tower earlier wasn't just a personal triumph; it was a deliberate provocation—a symbolic gesture that sent ripples through the fabric of a society long obsessed with order. With each drop of rain that hit her face, she felt a renewed sense of purpose. "This," she thought bitterly, "is the first of many signals that the old guard's grip is weakening." The risk she had taken, the calculated gamble of defying gravity and convention, was a stark reminder that innovation was born not of caution, but of daring—a willingness to sacrifice the illusion of safety for the uncertain, thrilling prospect of true change.

In the days that followed, the echoes of that rebellious act reverberated throughout Luminex. Corporate towers, once untouchable bastions of sanitised perfection, now bore subtle marks of dissent. A single spray-painted slogan on a window—a defiant "Vice Ignites"—became the spark that ignited a series of clandestine protests and creative interventions. The streets were awash with these subtle yet potent symbols, each one a silent challenge to the oppressive norms that had long held sway over the city.

And so, as the rain eventually subsided and the neon lights gave way to the harsh clarity of dawn, the rebels returned to their lives with a quiet but unyielding confidence. They had tasted the intoxicating power of risk, seen firsthand how vice could serve as the catalyst for innovation, and understood that every act of defiance was a step toward reclaiming a society that had long forgotten its own heartbeat. The basement meeting, the secret demonstrations, the whispered ideas in darkened corridors—these were the seeds of change, carefully nurtured in the shadows of Luminex.

In the quiet aftermath, while many in the city still clung to their comfortable illusions of safety and order, a growing number of citizens began to question the very foundation of their world. The lines between vice and virtue, once drawn in stark contrast, began to blur under the weight of lived experience. People started to see that the vices they had been taught to despise were, in fact, the raw materials of transformation. The grit of imperfection, the spark of defiance, and the unyielding courage to embrace risk—all of these were the ingredients of a new, dynamic culture that rejected sterile perfection in favour of authentic innovation.

As dusk approached once again, and the city of Luminex prepared to don its mask of neon splendour for another night, the revolution that had been kindled in that basement began to take on a life of its own. The rebels, driven by the bitter realisation that the only path to true change was paved with risk, continued to push the boundaries of what was possible. They knew that every new act of defiance, every bold experiment in the realm of vice, would reverberate far beyond their own lives—igniting a slow, inevitable shift in the collective consciousness of the city.

Thus, the catalyst of change had been set in motion. The dark allure of risk, the siren call of chaos, had become not a vice to be hidden away, but a potent force for innovation. And in the secret meetings, the whispered ideas, and the fearless acts of rebellion, the citizens of Luminex discovered a profound truth: that to ignite true progress, one must first be willing to embrace the dark, unpredictable, and beautifully dangerous side of life.

In the wake of that fateful, rain-soaked night, as the echoes of rebellious defiance continued to ripple through the darkened arteries of Luminex, the seeds sown in that underground basement began to germinate in unexpected corners of the city. The manifesto, once a mere whisper in the corridors of The Crucible, now reverberated off crumbling brick and gleaming glass alike, as if the city itself had caught the fever of audacity. It wasn't long before the very fabric of Luminex started to twist and buckle under the pressure of its own hypocrisy.

In a dilapidated warehouse near the edge of the industrial district, a new meeting had been called. The atmosphere was electric, charged with anticipation and the heady scent of rebellion that came from knowing one's every breath was an act of defiance. Mara arrived once again, her eyes glinting with the excitement of a conspirator who knew that each day was a chance to upend the oppressive status quo. This time, however, the discussion was not merely about individual exploits—it was about harnessing their collective energy to transform the very infrastructure of their society.

The group had grown since that first basement meeting, a motley assemblage of disenchanted intellectuals, underground artists, and renegade technologists who had all come to see that risk was the key to innovation. Among the new faces was Rina, a young architect whose designs rejected sterile modernity in favour of chaotic, organic forms. Rina spoke with quite fervour about the need to break free from the rigid blueprints of the past. "Architecture isn't about creating monuments to control," she declared, her voice soft but resolute, "it's about sculpting spaces that reflect our unpredictable, messy lives. When we let go of perfection, we invite creativity to flow through every crack and crevice." Her words, earnest and cutting, seemed to capture the essence of their shared struggle—the understanding that true innovation required not just a rejection of the old but a fearless embrace of the unknown.

As the discussion unfolded, Silas, whose enigmatic presence had become synonymous with the movement, offered his perspective on how risk could be institutionalised in the very mechanisms of power. "Our system," he began slowly, choosing each word with deliberate care, "has been designed to reward compliance and punish deviation. Yet, every institution, no matter how rigid, has its breaking point. If we can inject a dose of chaos into the heart of these structures, we force them to evolve, to adapt, to become more resilient in the face of human unpredictability." His eyes swept across the gathered faces, each one reflecting the shared conviction that the status quo was not invulnerable. "We have the power to remould our institutions—not by dismantling them outright, but by infusing them with the spirit of risk. In doing so, we reclaim the future for those of us who dare to live on the edge."

Marisol, the technologist with a reputation for turning disorder into digital breakthroughs, chimed in with her latest prototype—a decentralised platform designed to disrupt the rigid hierarchies of data control. "Imagine," she said, her tone imbued with both sarcasm and genuine excitement, "a system where data isn't filtered through the sterile pipelines of corporate interests, but flows freely, chaotic and unedited, like the raw pulse of the city itself." She demonstrated her creation with a flourish that drew a murmur of admiration from the group. "This platform doesn't rely on algorithms trained on sanitised, predictable inputs. It thrives on the unpredictability, the 'noise' that others discard as irrelevant. And from that noise, it extracts insights that are anything but ordinary." Her words painted a picture of a future where innovation was decentralised, unpredictable, and—most importantly—authentically human.

Outside, the city was slowly morphing in response to these ideas. In neighbourhoods once suffocated by the oppressive pursuit of perfection, clandestine murals began to appear overnight. Painted in bold, defiant strokes, these works of art transformed bleak walls into vibrant canvases of subversion. Each mural was a silent proclamation that vice was not something to be hidden away, but a vital ingredient in the alchemy of change. A particularly striking piece, splashed across the side of an old factory, read simply: "Risk Liberates." The words, rendered in jagged letters and dripping with defiant colour, served as a rallying cry for all who had grown tired of the sanitised narratives imposed by the elite.

In the midst of these changes, Theo found himself wrestling with a profound internal transformation. Having spent countless nights in the refuge of his cluttered apartment, pouring his heart and soul into ink-stained pages, he began to see that the chaotic beauty of risk was not merely an abstract concept but a lived reality. One rainy evening, as thunder rumbled in the distance and the city shuddered under the weight of an approaching storm, he sat by his window, notebook in hand, and wrote feverishly. His words, raw and unfiltered, captured the tension between fear and desire—a recognition that the very act of risking everything was both terrifying and exhilarating. "To embrace risk," he scribbled, "is to open oneself to a universe of possibilities. It is to shatter the illusion of safety and discover that in the fragments of our broken selves lie the seeds of true innovation." Each line of his poem was a testament to the transformation taking root in his soul—a journey from the sterile confines of a predetermined life to the uncharted territory of genuine self-discovery.

As the hours slipped by and the storm outside subsided into a melancholic drizzle, the rebels reconvened once more in a refurbished loft that had become the new nerve centre for their movement. The space was a riot of colour and sound—a juxtaposition of salvaged furniture, improvised art installations, and a cacophony of voices all united by the belief that vice, in its most honest form, was the birthplace of change. Here, amidst the backdrop of peeling wallpaper and mismatched cushions, the group began to draft a more comprehensive plan to infiltrate and disrupt the entrenched power structures of Luminex.

The discussion grew heated as visions clashed and ideas took on a life of their own. Rina presented sketches of radical, adaptive architecture that would allow public spaces to evolve organically—a design that celebrated impermanence and unpredictability. "Imagine," she said, her eyes sparkling with a dangerous kind of hope, "buildings that breathe, that change shape according to the whims of the people. A structure that isn't defined by rigid lines, but by the dynamic interplay of light, shadow, and human emotion." Her proposals, though seemingly fantastical, were met with nods of enthusiasm from a group that had long been starving for a taste of the extraordinary.

Silas, ever the voice of measured rebellion, argued that the transformation of physical spaces was only half the battle. "We need to rewire our social networks as well," he declared, his voice resonating with the calm authority of one who had seen the inner workings of power. "True change is not just about what we build, but how we connect. Our existing networks are designed to filter and sanitise information—to keep us in a bubble of curated consensus. We must create alternative channels, where ideas can circulate freely, unburdened by the constraints of censorship and corporate control." His vision was both radical and deceptively simple: a web of underground communities connected by shared values and unfiltered truth—a network as unpredictable and vibrant as the city itself.

Marisol, never one to be outdone, unveiled a prototype for a new kind of communication platform that would allow these networks to flourish without the heavy hand of regulation. "This isn't just another social media tool," she explained, her voice laced with both irony and passion. "It's an open forum where every voice, every dissenting opinion, is amplified rather than muted. In a world where data is curated to preserve an illusion of order, our platform will be a sanctuary for the raw, unedited pulse of humanity. Here, the chaotic beauty of free expression will be celebrated as the engine of innovation." The group marvelled at the potential of her creation—a digital space that promised to disrupt the carefully controlled narratives of the mainstream.

As the night deepened into the early hours of morning, the rebels of Luminex began to realise that their movement was no longer confined to isolated meetings and secret gatherings. Their ideas, once whispered in the dark, had started to permeate every facet of the city. The once impenetrable walls of corporate control now bore the scars of subversive art and the indelible marks of dissent. Every act of risk, every bold experiment with vice, was a stroke on the canvas of a reimagined future—a future where innovation was born not from the sanitised corridors of power but from the chaotic energy of lived experience.

In that loft, as the first light of dawn crept through grimy windows and cast fractured patterns on the floor, the rebels gathered in a quiet moment of reflection. Their eyes, red-rimmed from sleepless nights and charged with the fervour of revolution, met one another in a shared understanding that what they were doing was bigger than any one individual. They were rewriting the rules of a city that had long demanded perfection, challenging every assumption about what it meant to be modern, to be innovative, to be truly alive.

Rina, her voice soft and reflective, summed up the sentiment that had been building all night. "We are the spark in a dark world," she said, "and every act of rebellion, every risk we take, is a flicker of light that can ignite a blaze. We are not here to build a new order from scratch, but to tear down the old one and let the chaos of life fill the void with something real and raw." Her words, though gentle, carried the weight of undeniable truth—a promise that in the art of risk lay the seeds of genuine transformation.

For Theo, the night's discussions had crystallised into a singular realisation: that risk was the silent pulse of creativity, the unsung hero of every breakthrough. He resolved, as he scribbled yet another line in his ever-growing notebook, that he would no longer shy away from the dangerous edges of his own ideas. Instead, he would dive headfirst into the tumultuous sea of possibility, embracing every fall and every failure as necessary steps on the road to authentic innovation.

As the dawn matured into a bright, unyielding day, the rebels dispersed back into the labyrinth of Luminex. The manifesto they had begun to draft in that loft—a living document of subversive ideas and dark aspirations—was slated for further refinement in the coming days. They knew that their movement, fueled by the potent allure of risk, was still in its infancy. Yet even in these early moments, the impact of their defiance was unmistakable. Across the city, the boundaries between vice and virtue were starting to blur, as ordinary citizens began to question the sanitised narratives that had long been their only reality.

In a small café on a busy street, an office worker paused over his lukewarm coffee as he noticed a new piece of graffiti on the wall—a scrawled declaration in bold, rebellious letters: "Innovation Lives in Chaos." The words stirred something inside him, a faint echo of a truth he had long suppressed. And though he returned to his day with the mundane rhythm of corporate routine, that brief moment of clarity lingered like a secret promise—an acknowledgment that beneath the polished surface of his world lay an untapped reservoir of raw, unfiltered possibility.

Back in the underground, the conversation continued well into the morning. Silas, with his trademark calm, spoke of the inevitable resistance that awaited them as they pushed their vision further into the light. "Change," he remarked, "is never accepted without struggle. The forces of conformity will claw at every inch of our progress, but that is the very nature of evolution. Our risk, our embrace of chaos—it is what forces the old order to crumble, even if just a little, every day." His words, measured and patient, were a rallying call to all who had gathered—a reminder that every revolutionary act, no matter how small, was a blow against the inertia of a stagnant society.

As the morning sun climbed higher, casting long shadows across the city's shattered facades, the rebels of Luminex began to disperse once more. Each carried with them the tangible weight of a night spent challenging the impossible, their minds alive with ideas that promised to reshape a world built on lies. They knew that the road ahead would be fraught with setbacks and that the forces of the old order would not relinquish their grip without a fight. Yet in their hearts burned a fierce conviction—that in every risk taken, in every vice embraced as a tool for change, lay the potential to spark an innovation that could transform not just Luminex, but the very nature of progress itself was irrevocably altered that day. In the moments following the clandestine meetings, as ideas flowed freely and the rebels of Luminex began to reshape the way they saw the world, a quiet, almost imperceptible shift began to take root. It started as a tremor in the concrete—a subtle breaking of barriers, a fissure in the old order that had long stifled creativity. The seeds of subversion, sown in the dank corners of forgotten warehouses and whispered in the dim glow of neon-lit basements, now pushed upward toward the light of a new dawn.

In the labyrinthine alleyways of Luminex, the very walls seemed to pulse with rebellious energy. Murals sprang forth overnight on crumbling brick surfaces—vivid depictions of broken chains, shattered masks, and defiant slogans that read like a manifesto of unapologetic truth. "Embrace Chaos," one mural proclaimed in jagged, spray-painted letters. "Let Risk Reign." These were not mere acts of vandalism; they were declarations that the sanitised narratives of the elite were no longer absolute. Each stroke of paint was a direct challenge to a society that had, for too long, equated perfection with value.

Mara, whose audacious exploits had become legendary among the underground circles, found herself both exhilarated and contemplative in these early hours. Standing on a fire escape that overlooked a sprawling plaza now adorned with subversive art, she allowed herself a moment of rare introspection. The adrenaline from her earlier climb still coursed through her veins, but now it was tempered by a sober realisation: their acts of defiance were only the beginning. Every daring move, every calculated risk taken in the name of liberation, was not just a personal victory—it was a spark that ignited collective change.

She recalled the thrill of scaling that glass tower, the taste of rain on her lips, and the moment her banner unfurled in the stormy sky. That act was more than symbolic; it was a repudiation of the false security the corporate bastions had sold to the masses. In that moment, risk had become a tool—a weapon to dismantle the oppressive constructs of order. Mara's mind raced with possibilities: if one act could inspire a mural, what other barriers could be shattered if the spirit of rebellion spread like wildfire? She knew that the path ahead was treacherous, that the forces of conformity would tighten their grip in response, but she also knew that change could only come when people were willing to flirt with danger, to embrace the uncertain, and to revel in the imperfections that made them human.

Down on the street, Theo trudged along rain-slicked sidewalks, his notebook clutched tightly to his chest as though it were a talisman. Each step he took was measured, each reflection in the puddles a reminder that the city was transforming before his eyes. He had spent countless nights at The Crucible, scribbling lines of poetry that captured the raw tension between order and chaos. Now, as he walked amidst a city that was slowly awakening to the promise of a new era, his thoughts turned to the intimate dance between risk and reward. He remembered the fervent debates in the loft, the passion with which his comrades spoke of dismantling sanitised narratives, and the bitter beauty of realising that true art was born from the tumult of failure.

Theo's mind wandered to the young idealist, Julian, whose wide-eyed wonder had gradually given way to a hardened resolve. Julian had once argued that risk was nothing more than reckless abandon—a folly that left one vulnerable to the caprices of fate. But through the relentless assault of lived experience and the piercing critiques of his peers, Julian had begun to understand that every moment of daring was a deliberate act of creation. "We are not defined by the absence of fear," Theo had written in his notebook during one of those long nights, "but by the courage to defy it, to turn every misstep into a brushstroke on the canvas of our lives." Now, as he observed the graffiti and the spontaneous gatherings unfolding in unexpected corners of Luminex, he felt that same transformative power stirring within him—a deep, resonant conviction that risk was the only path to a future unburdened by the constraints of imposed perfection.

Elsewhere, in a repurposed storefront that had become a haven for subversive thought, the rebels continued to solidify their plans. Rina, the young architect with a penchant for designs that celebrated impermanence, led a workshop that brought together artists, engineers, and activists. The space was cluttered with sketches, blueprints, and makeshift models of buildings that defied gravity and conventional aesthetics. Rina's voice carried a quiet intensity as she explained her vision: "Imagine a city that isn't built to last, but built to evolve. Structures that breathe, that adapt to the chaotic rhythm of human life. Perfection is static; we are dynamic, and our environments must reflect that truth." Her words, delivered with a blend of hopeful idealism and defiant sarcasm, sparked vigorous discussions among the group. Some argued that such radical ideas were nothing more than dreams too grand to materialise, while others, their eyes alight with conviction, saw in them the blueprint for a revolution in urban design—a rebellion against sterile architecture and the oppressive uniformity of corporate skylines.

At the same time, Silas and Marisol worked feverishly behind the scenes, their minds merging technology and art to create tools that could disrupt the very systems that perpetuated mediocrity. Silas, ever the philosopher of rebellion, envisioned a network—an underground communication platform that would bypass the sanitised channels of mainstream media. "We need a digital sanctuary," he argued one night as he meticulously coded amidst the flickering light of a single, steadfast bulb. "A space where raw, unedited truth flows like wildfire, where every dissenting voice is amplified rather than muted. It's in the uncontrolled data—the so-called 'noise'—that we will find the seeds of a new narrative." Marisol, with her uncanny knack for turning chaos into code, worked to refine this platform, her fingers dancing over the keyboard in a frenzied yet deliberate rhythm. She knew that by dismantling the filters and constraints imposed by the corporate gatekeepers, they could unleash a torrent of unadulterated ideas—a digital revolt that mirrored the physical insurgency taking shape on the streets.

As these projects unfolded, the ripple effects of the rebellion began to permeate the broader culture of Luminex. Ordinary citizens, long numbed by the monotony of routine, started to question the rigid boundaries of their existence. In coffee shops and on crowded bus stops, whispered conversations sparked debates about the true cost of safety and the hidden virtues of imperfection. A middle-aged office worker, who had once worn his tailored suit as armour against a world of uncertainty, found himself inexplicably drawn to a mural emblazoned with the words "Risk Liberates." That simple, defiant message chipped away at the carefully constructed illusions of order, igniting a flicker of doubt in his otherwise complacent heart. Slowly, he began to see that the controlled life he had accepted as normal was nothing more than a gilded cage—one that stifled his capacity for genuine expression and left him adrift in a sea of unfulfilled potential.

In the vibrant chaos of Luminex's underground, the rebels pressed forward with their vision of a future built on the raw power of vice and risk. Their manifesto, once a whispered promise in a smoke-filled room, was now evolving into a clarion call that resonated across the city. Meetings were held in secret, in places that defied the sterile uniformity of conventional spaces—a dilapidated library here, an abandoned subway station there. Everywhere, the conversation was the same: that the old order, with its relentless pursuit of perfection, was fundamentally flawed. The very elements that had been scorned as vice—chaos, imperfection, unpredictability—were now being recognised as the wellspring of true innovation.

One particularly memorable evening, a gathering was held in an overgrown courtyard behind a derelict building. Lanterns fashioned from discarded metal and plastic cast flickering, eerie glows on the assembled crowd. Among the attendees was a seasoned street performer named Marco, whose life had been a tapestry of risk and rebellion. With a voice both mellifluous and biting, Marco recounted the story of how he had once risked everything on a single, fateful performance. "I was offered a chance to join a prestigious troupe," he recalled, his tone laced with bitter irony, "but I knew that accepting their sanitised version of art would be like signing my own death warrant. Instead, I took to the streets, risking exposure, humiliation, and rejection—yet every moment of that raw, unfiltered existence was a victory over conformity." His tale, punctuated by bursts of laughter and pained silences, was a reminder that the courage to embrace risk was the truest measure of one's authenticity.

As the rebels continued to exchange ideas, debate strategies, and plan future interventions, the atmosphere grew charged with a palpable sense of purpose. The manifesto was evolving—its pages filled with the voices of those who had dared to challenge the status quo. It was no longer a single, monolithic document but a living, breathing testament to the power of collective defiance. Every new contribution, every freshly scrawled line of bitter truth, was a brick in the foundation of a movement that sought to dismantle the old guard and usher in a new era of unvarnished reality.

Back at the heart of this insurgency, Theo's poetic musings began to crystallise into a series of definitive works—a body of literature that captured the tumult of this transformative period. His words, once confined to the margins of his notebook, now began to find their way into underground publications and digital forums. "In every reckless act, there is a beauty," he wrote in one passage, "for it is only when we surrender to the chaos that we unearth the hidden depths of our soul." His verses resonated with a generation that had grown weary of the endless pursuit of sterile ideals—a generation that had learned, through bitter experience, that the only way to truly live was to risk it all.

And so, as days turned into weeks and weeks into months, the movement grew. What had begun as a series of isolated acts of rebellion now coalesced into a powerful, almost unstoppable force. The rebels of Luminex had ignited a spark—a spark that spread through the city like wildfire, consuming the old structures of power and giving rise to something new, something undeniably raw and real. The corporate towers and pristine plazas, once symbols of unassailable order, were now interspersed with bold, defiant graffiti and pop-up exhibitions that celebrated the chaos of human experience.

Yet, even as the movement gained momentum, the forces of conformity were not idle. The powers-that-be, threatened by the growing unrest, began to tighten their grip. Increased surveillance, more aggressive censorship, and a renewed propaganda campaign were deployed in an effort to reassert control. But these measures only served to underscore the absurdity of their mission. For every attempt to muzzle dissent, a hundred more voices rose in defiant chorus. The very tools of repression became fuel for the rebellion—a perverse irony that the sanitised tactics of the elite only accelerated the transformation they so desperately sought to prevent.

In quiet boardrooms and opulent offices high above the tumult of the streets, executives and bureaucrats scrambled to explain away the insurgent symbolism that now decorated every corner of the city. Reports were filed, press releases issued, and public statements crafted with all the sterile precision of a machine. But beneath the polished surface of their controlled narratives, there was an undeniable tremor of uncertainty—a recognition that the rebellion was not just a passing fad, but a seismic shift in the cultural and social fabric of Luminex.

As Part 3 of Chapter 5 unfolds, it is clear that the catalyst of change—fueled by vice, risk, and the audacious spirit of the rebels—was reshaping not only the physical landscape of the city but also the very minds of its citizens. In every whispered conversation in a crowded café, in every defiant mural splashed across a gray wall, there was a shared understanding that the old world, with its promise of perfection, was a lie. The truth lay in the imperfections, the risks taken, and the unyielding determination to live authentically.

In the back alleys and abandoned corners of Luminex, where the forgotten and the defiant gathered, the revolution was quietly, inexorably unfolding. It was a revolution not of violence or chaos in the conventional sense, but of ideas—ideas that challenged every assumption about what was possible, every rule that had long been held sacrosanct. The rebels understood that the path to a future defined by true innovation was paved with risk. They celebrated every act of daring as a necessary step in the evolution of society, a rejection of the false promises of order and control.

Mara, Theo, Rina, Silas, Marisol, and all those who had joined this movement now looked to the horizon with a mixture of fierce determination and weary acceptance. They knew that the battle ahead would be long and arduous, that the forces of conformity would not easily relinquish their hold. But they also knew that the stakes were nothing less than the soul of their city—the very essence of what it meant to be alive in a world that had long celebrated the sterile and the perfect at the expense of the beautifully real.

In the weeks and months that followed, the movement continued to evolve. Underground art shows, spontaneous street performances, and guerrilla installations became commonplace, each one a testament to the unbridled creativity that risk had unleashed. The digital platform developed by Marisol and Silas grew steadily, becoming a virtual haven for dissenters and visionaries alike. It was a space where raw, unedited truth could flourish, unburdened by the filters and fictions of the mainstream. And with every new post, every viral video that captured a moment of unrestrained defiance, the collective consciousness of Luminex began to shift—a slow, inexorable movement toward a future that embraced the chaotic beauty of imperfection.

The transformation was subtle yet profound. In the corridors of power, whispers of rebellion were met with attempts at control, but they could not silence the persistent murmur of a society awakened. Ordinary citizens, who had once accepted the sanitised version of their lives, began to see that every act of rebellion—no matter how small—was a victory against the tyranny of conformity. In classrooms, at bus stops, and even in the quiet solitude of late-night commutes, the message of the rebellion seeped into everyday conversations. It was a message that celebrated risk, that honoured the messy, unpredictable nature of human existence, and that dared to ask: What if imperfection were the true measure of beauty?

And so, as the movement forged ahead, the rebels of Luminex carried their manifesto like a banner—a banner that declared, with all the dark sarcasm and unyielding passion of those who had tasted the bitter sweetness of risk, that the future belonged not to the cautious or the sanitised, but to those who were willing to risk it all. The legacy of their rebellion was etched not in grand proclamations or sweeping gestures, but in the countless moments of defiance that had reshaped a city. Every daring act, every unscripted moment of chaos, was a reminder that progress was born in the crucible of risk and that true innovation emerged from the dark spaces where imperfection reigned supreme.

As the sun climbed higher over Luminex and the rebel gatherings slowly dispersed into the daily grind, the echoes of that transformative night remained. The scars on the city's walls, the defiant words sprayed in alleys, and the raw poetry scrawled in digital forums served as constant reminders that the movement was alive and evolving. And within the hearts of those who dared to dream, there burned an unquenchable fire—a fire fuelled by the certainty that the price of real change was the willingness to embrace risk, to defy expectations, and to celebrate every imperfect, audacious moment of existence.

In that dark, turbulent landscape, where vice had become the catalyst of innovation, the rebels of Luminex had not only challenged the old order—they had redefined it. They had shown that progress was not the domain of the sanitised or the safe, but belonged to the brave, to those who recognised that in every act of risk lay the potential to rewrite the future. And as the movement continued its inexorable march forward, every defiant act, every whispered manifesto, and every piece of rebellious art contributed to a mosaic of change—a mosaic that, piece by piece, was reshaping the very identity of a city that had long been stifled by the tyranny of perfection.

Thus, as the day wore on and the rebels dispersed into the bustling chaos of everyday life, the impact of their actions resonated far beyond the confines of their secret meetings. The air in Luminex was charged with a new energy—a sense that the very fabric of reality was being rewoven with threads of risk, rebellion, and raw, unfiltered creativity. And even as the forces of conformity struggled to reassert their control, the spirit of the revolution could not be contained. For in every daring act, in every bold statement painted on a crumbling wall, the rebels had carved a permanent reminder into the heart of the city: that the future was not dictated by sterile routines or safe choices, but by the relentless, unpredictable power of those who dared to embrace the dark allure of risk.

But the revolution was not content to merely whisper its defiance in hidden corners. As the insurgency matured, the once-impenetrable bastions of corporate power began to tremble under the weight of relentless, subversive artistry and the ever-growing chorus of dissent. In the days that followed the stormy nights of rebellion, the pulse of risk and vice seeped deeper into the very bones of Luminex. Every crumbling façade, every hastily scrawled slogan on a drab office window, was a reminder that the old order was cracking—fracturing beneath the relentless pressure of a movement that had grown far beyond its humble beginnings.

In a refurbished loft turned strategic war room, the rebels gathered once more. The air was heavy with the scent of stale coffee, sweat, and the palpable tension of impending change. Maps of the city, splattered with vivid graffiti and annotated with cryptic notes, covered one wall. On another, whiteboards overflowed with plans for guerrilla interventions, digital strategies, and proposals for urban reengineering. Faces lit by the pale glow of computer screens and the erratic flicker of neon outside bore the marks of sleepless nights and fierce determination. Here, in this crucible of chaos and possibility, ideas were not merely discussed—they were weaponised.

Mara, her eyes alight with that unmistakable spark of rebellious fire, addressed the group. "We've seen how a single act—a banner unfurled on a glass tower—can shatter illusions. But we're not here to stop at isolated stunts. We need to keep the pressure on, to let every corner of this city know that risk is the new norm." Her tone, a blend of sardonic humour and unyielding conviction, cut through the murmur like a siren's call. "Every mural, every act of defiant graffiti, every hacked billboard—it's all a part of a mosaic that we're building. A mosaic that shows the world exactly what it means to be unashamedly, unapologetically human."

Across the room, Rina, the visionary architect with dreams of adaptive, living structures, leaned forward, her fingers tracing the outline of a hastily drawn concept. "Imagine if our public spaces could evolve organically," she proposed, her voice both gentle and insistent. "Buildings that aren't static monuments of corporate greed but living, breathing entities that change with the people who use them. If we can prove that chaos is not our enemy but our creative ally, then we can force our oppressors to acknowledge that the old blueprints—both literal and metaphorical—are obsolete." Her words were met with enthusiastic nods and murmurs of agreement. The notion of dynamic, unpredictable design wasn't merely radical—it was a direct challenge to the sterile, unchanging skyline that had long dominated Luminex.

Meanwhile, Silas and Marisol continued their tireless work on their digital platform. In a cluttered corner of the loft, Silas's calm, deliberate fingers danced over a keyboard as lines of unfiltered code began to form a system that could bypass the mainstream's sanitised data channels. "Our goal," he explained in a low, measured tone to an attentive Marisol, "is to create a space where raw information flows unhindered—a digital underground that mirrors the chaotic beauty of our physical rebellion. It must be a sanctuary for every voice that's been silenced by the polished lies of the corporate machine." Marisol, eyes fixed on her screen, replied, "Every byte of data that flows through our network will be a fragment of the unedited truth. We're not interested in curated perfection; we want the messy, unpredictable reality. That's where innovation lives." The urgency in their collaboration was palpable—each keystroke a deliberate act of defiance against the sanitised narratives imposed by those in power.

Outside the loft, Luminex itself was undergoing a quiet metamorphosis. The relentless hum of surveillance cameras and the calculated routines of corporate life were slowly being overlaid with the unpredictable rhythms of rebellion. Ordinary citizens—once complacent in their routine—began to notice the subtle changes. At a crowded bus stop, an office worker in a crisp suit paused as he noticed a newly painted slogan on the wall: "Imperfection is Our Revolution." The phrase, scrawled in erratic, vibrant letters, jolted him from his autopilot existence. For a fleeting moment, he wondered what it might mean to live without the constant pressure to conform—to dare to risk a little, to embrace a fragment of the unpredictable.

In a busy café downtown, the atmosphere was charged with a subtle, disquieting energy. Regular patrons, who had long sipped their lattes in quiet resignation, now exchanged furtive glances over the rim of coffee cups as they discussed the sudden appearance of underground zines. These pamphlets—printed in hasty runs and filled with the raw, unpolished poetry of the resistance—had begun to circulate among the people. One zine bore the title "Chaos Over

Order," a declaration that resonated with anyone who had ever felt the crushing weight of societal expectations. As these small, rebellious artifacts passed from hand to hand, they carried with them the promise of a new way of seeing the world—a world where the pursuit of perfection was no longer the highest virtue, and where every risk taken was a triumph in its own right.

Back in the loft, the rebels' discussions deepened as the day wore on. A heated debate ensued over the question of how best to confront the oppressive institutions that had long maintained their grip on power. "We could stage more public interventions," proposed one of the younger activists, his voice trembling with both excitement and fear. "Take over a billboard, hack into a live broadcast, flood the digital airwaves with our manifesto." His suggestion was met with a mixture of enthusiasm and caution—every act of public defiance carried with it the risk of harsh retaliation, yet the potential payoff was immeasurable. "The key," Mara interjected with a wry smile, "is to strike when they least expect it. Our power lies in the element of surprise, in our ability to disrupt their comfortable illusions before they have time to react."

The conversation gradually turned to the nature of risk itself—a concept that had evolved from a mere tactic into a philosophy that underpinned every decision they made. Theo, whose poetic reflections had already begun to circulate on underground blogs and digital forums, spoke softly but firmly: "Risk is not the absence of caution—it is the acknowledgement that to live fully, we must be willing to embrace uncertainty. Each time we step beyond the safe, sterile boundaries of what is expected, we open ourselves to the possibility of failure. But it is in that failure—raw, unedited, and sometimes bitter—that true innovation is born." His words, steeped in the melancholic wisdom of one who had seen both the heights of hope and the depths of despair, resonated deeply with the group. They were not naive; they understood that every act of rebellion carried with it a price. Yet they also knew that the price of inaction—the eternal, suffocating weight of conformity—was far greater.

As the discussion wound down and the rebels began to disperse, the loft fell into a contemplative silence punctuated only by the soft hum of computers and the distant murmur of the city. Each member of the movement left with a renewed sense of purpose, aware that they were at the cusp of something monumental. The manifesto they had been drafting—a living, breathing document of raw ideas and unfiltered truths—was nearly complete, a testament to the power of collective risk. In its pages, every whispered idea, every moment of doubt transformed into defiance, had been meticulously recorded. It was more than a call to arms; it was an invitation to a new way of life, one where the unpredictable dance of risk was celebrated as the true engine of progress.

Later that evening, as the sun dipped below the horizon and the city was bathed in the cold, indifferent glow of neon, Mara and Theo met once again atop a modest rooftop overlooking a maze of congested streets and towering office blocks. The air was cool, and the distant sound of sirens mingled with the steady rhythm of the urban night. Mara took a long, contemplative drag from a cigarette, exhaling a plume of smoke that mingled with the neon haze. "We've set something in motion," she observed quietly, her voice tinged with both satisfaction and melancholy. "Every act of risk, every defiant symbol—it's like a small rebellion that, over time, will coalesce into a force that can topple these tired structures." Theo nodded, his gaze fixed on the horizon where the city's sharp outlines blurred into a riot of light and shadow. "We're not just breaking rules," he replied softly, "we're rewriting them. And if that means we have to live on the edge forever, then so be it."

Their conversation drifted into silence, each lost in thought as the city around them pulsed with the uncertain promise of change. Down below, the repercussions of their movement were already being felt. In corporate offices, executives exchanged worried glances as reports of defiant graffiti and unauthorised digital broadcasts began to flood their secure networks. In quiet suburban neighbourhoods, parents whispered anxiously about the strange new slogans that had appeared on public benches and street signs.

The controlled world of sanitised perfection was cracking, and with each fissure, the rebels' message of risk and authenticity spread further.

In the coming days, the pressure on the old order mounted. The authorities, desperate to quell the growing unrest, increased their surveillance and tightened restrictions on public gatherings. Yet every measure they took to silence dissent only fanned the flames of rebellion higher. Underground workshops sprang up in abandoned buildings, and secret meetings in dingy backrooms became more frequent. The digital platform that Silas and Marisol had built blossomed into a thriving community where every new idea was shared with a mix of urgency and defiant humour. The citizens of Luminex, tired of the monotonous hum of controlled existence, began to emerge from the shadows, drawn by the promise of a future that celebrated their very imperfections.

For the rebels, risk was no longer just an abstract concept—it was a daily, living reality. Every challenge, every confrontation with the forces of conformity, reinforced their belief that the true path to progress was paved with uncertainty and audacity. And in the quiet moments between skirmishes, when the adrenaline faded and the true cost of defiance set in, they found solace in the knowledge that they were part of something far greater than themselves—a revolution that would one day reshape the world in the image of raw, unedited truth.

Thus, as dusk once again draped its inky veil over Luminex, the movement marched forward—step by defiant step, act by calculated act. In every corner of the city, from the high-rise towers of the corporate elite to the forgotten alleys of the underclass, the echoes of their rebellion grew louder. The legacy of risk, once scorned as a vice, had become the very catalyst of change—a reminder that innovation, in its truest form, was born not from the safety of predictability but from the courage to embrace the chaotic unknown.

And so, with hearts hardened by struggle yet softened by the undeniable beauty of imperfection, the rebels of Luminex stepped into the night. Their manifesto—an ever-evolving testament to the power of risk—was now more than just a document. It was a living, breathing force, a beacon for all those who dared to defy a world built on sterile routines. As they dispersed into the sprawling urban labyrinth, the message was clear: the future would be written not by those who played it safe, but by those bold enough to risk everything for a taste of the real, the raw, and the revolutionary.

But as the relentless pulse of rebellion continued to echo through the streets of Luminex, the underground movement reached a critical juncture—a moment when every whispered idea and every bold act of defiance was converging into something far greater than the sum of its parts. In the weeks following the explosive nights of subversion, the city had transformed, if only imperceptibly, into a living canvas painted with the scars and triumphs of risk. The once-sterile facades of corporate towers were now interlaced with vibrant slogans and rebellious art, each marking a silent revolt against a system that had long thrived on perfection and predictability.

In a crumbling building that had been repurposed into a community centre for the insurgents, the rebels gathered for what would become their most consequential meeting yet. The space was a riot of contrasting elements: salvaged furniture mixed with digital displays streaming unfiltered news from their underground network, walls adorned with provocative murals, and an atmosphere heavy with both anticipation and defiant camaraderie. It was here that the final draft of their manifesto—the living document that had been evolving over countless secret sessions—was to be completed. This manifesto was more than a call to arms; it was a declaration that risk, in all its dangerous glory, was the essential engine of progress.

Mara, whose exploits had become the stuff of legend, stood at the head of the assembly. Her eyes, fierce and unyielding, swept over the gathered crowd of misfits, idealists, and renegades. "We've come a long way," she began, her voice resonating with a blend of bitter irony and unbridled conviction. "What started as isolated acts of defiance, as solitary gestures against a suffocating order, has become a movement—a force that is slowly, but surely, tearing down the very foundations of this false paradise we call Luminex." There was a pause as she allowed the weight of her words to sink in. "Our message is simple: true innovation is born from risk. Perfection is a prison, and our imperfections—our audacity, our chaos—are the keys to a future that celebrates the raw, unedited truth of our existence."

The room erupted in murmurs of agreement, and as the meeting progressed, the rebels recounted their recent successes with a mixture of sardonic humour and wistful pride. Silas shared how their digital platform had begun to disrupt the sanitised data channels of the corporate elite, providing an unfiltered space where dissenting voices thrived like wildflowers in a cracked concrete jungle. Marisol chimed in with details about underground art exhibits that had erupted overnight on the sterile walls of high-rise offices—each mural a defiant middle finger raised at the notion of controlled perfection.

Rina, the visionary architect, presented her latest sketches for adaptive public spaces—structures that were designed to evolve organically with the rhythm of human life. "Imagine a city where buildings don't stand as monuments to static ambition," she explained, her voice a quiet blend of passion and practicality, "but rather as living entities that grow, adapt, and transform with the people who inhabit them. Our world is messy, unpredictable—and our architecture should reflect that reality." Her words, delivered with a calm intensity, resonated deeply with the audience, many of whom had long yearned for an environment that was as dynamic and unpredictable as they were.

Yet, amid the infectious optimism, there was also a palpable undercurrent of caution. The rebels knew that every step they took towards this radical vision of the future brought them closer to the wrath of the old order. Across Luminex, as the state increased surveillance and public authorities tightened their grip, a silent war was being waged—a war not of brute force but of ideas. In sleek boardrooms and pristine offices, the executives of the old regime scrambled to counter the insurgency with polished press releases and calculated crackdowns. But each move only served to amplify the rebels' message, turning every act of repression into a badge of honour for those daring enough to risk everything for authenticity.

In the community centre, as the meeting wore on, a young poet named Julian—whose transformation from a cautious idealist into a fervent revolutionary had been nothing short of dramatic—rose to speak. His voice, soft yet resolute, carried a wisdom that belied his years. "We live in a world that tells us to play it safe," he began, his eyes reflecting both youthful determination and the scars of hard-won experience. "But every time we choose the safe path, we resign ourselves to a life of quiet desperation. Risk isn't about being reckless—it's about being real. It's about choosing to see the beauty in our own chaos, the poetry in our failures. Only then can we truly shape a future that isn't just another sanitised copy of the past." His words, simple and profound, ignited a renewed sense of purpose among the rebels, reaffirming their belief that risk was not only necessary—it was revolutionary.

As the manifesto neared its final form, the discussion turned to the strategies for disseminating their message to the broader populace. Marisol outlined plans to integrate their digital platform with social media channels, creating a network that could bypass traditional censorship and amplify their voice. "Our platform isn't just for us," she declared, "it's for everyone who's ever felt trapped by the relentless pursuit of perfection. It's a digital battleground where raw, unfiltered truth can flourish without the chains of corporate manipulation." The enthusiasm in the room was electric, and it was clear that the rebels were poised to extend their influence far beyond the underground enclaves of Luminex.

Outside, the city was awakening to a new reality. The rebellious slogans that had once adorned the dark corners of back alleys were now becoming common sight on the sidewalks of bustling neighbourhoods. In a small suburban park, an elderly man paused by a bench to read a spray-painted message: "Dare to be Different."

The words, scrawled in bold, erratic letters, seemed to challenge the very core of his conditioned existence. For a fleeting moment, he looked around with a spark of recognition—a silent acknowledgment that perhaps the world was ready for a change, even if he wasn't quite sure what that change would entail.

Over the following days, the impact of the rebels' actions grew increasingly visible. The city's corporate titans, once invincible in their ivory towers, now found themselves grappling with a subtle but undeniable transformation. A series of unauthorised public art installations appeared overnight in the financial district, each piece a visual manifesto that celebrated imperfection and defied conventional beauty. The digital platform spearheaded by Silas and Marisol was gaining traction among citizens who were tired of the filtered, sanitised content fed to them by mainstream media. Every new post, every shared video of daring acts, contributed to an undercurrent of change that was impossible to ignore.

In quiet conversations in cafés and on crowded public transport, people began to whisper about the "risk revolution"—a term that had quickly spread among those who were beginning to see the allure of living authentically. They discussed the merits of a life unburdened by the constant pursuit of perfection, the joy that came from embracing failure as a stepping stone to growth. In this growing discourse, the rebels' manifesto was cited not as a radical treatise for a fringe minority, but as a source of inspiration for anyone who dared to question the status quo.

One particularly poignant moment came during an impromptu street performance in a busy intersection near the central business district. A group of young artists, armed with nothing but spray cans and makeshift instruments, staged a performance that transformed the drab, gray expanse into a dynamic celebration of imperfection. They rapped and chanted in a biting, sarcastic tone, their lyrics painting a vivid picture of a world where risk was celebrated as the true mark of innovation. "You can cage us in your ivory towers," one of them declared, his voice echoing off the glass and steel of nearby offices, "but you can't cage our hearts. We live for the risk, for the chaos—'cause that's where we find our truth." The performance drew a crowd, and for those few minutes, the boundary between the rebel underground and the everyday citizen blurred, as even the most skeptical onlookers found themselves nodding in agreement, caught up in the infectious energy of the moment.

Back at the community centre, as the final words of the manifesto were penned and the meeting drew to a close, a deep sense of collective purpose filled the room. Every rebel, every misfit, felt that they were part of something monumental—an irreversible tide of change that would one day sweep away the oppressive remnants of a society built on sterile perfection. They knew that the road ahead would be fraught with challenges, that the forces of conformity would strike back with all the might of a desperate regime. But they also knew that their movement, rooted in the radical embrace of risk and vice, was built on an unassailable truth: that innovation, in its purest form, could only emerge from the brave, unfiltered chaos of human imperfection.

As the meeting adjourned and the rebels dispersed into the labyrinthine streets of Luminex, the manifesto was lifted from paper into the realm of legend. Its ideas were already taking root in the hearts of those who had grown weary of a world that prized safety over authenticity. In every spray-painted wall, every whispered conversation in a subway car, the message was clear: risk is not the enemy, but the lifeblood of progress. And in that truth lay the promise of a future where every imperfect, rebellious act could spark a revolution of innovation—a future where the dark allure of vice would be recognised not as a vice at all, but as the most potent catalyst for change.

In the ensuing weeks, as the digital platform and underground art proliferated, Luminex began to feel the tremors of transformation. The rebel network expanded beyond the narrow confines of the disaffected underground, reaching into neighbourhoods and communities that had long resigned themselves to the oppressive predictability of modern life. A new wave of public discourse emerged, one that celebrated risk, questioned the old hierarchies, and embraced the beauty of a chaotic, imperfect world. The city's old order, though still clinging to its brittle constructs of control, could no longer ignore the rising chorus of dissent.

On a crisp evening as the neon lights flickered on and the city prepared once more to don its mask of sanitised perfection, a final rally was held at a long-abandoned public square. Thousands of citizens gathered, drawn by rumours of a spontaneous event that promised to shake the very foundations of their existence. Amid the throng, the rebels—Mara, Theo, Rina, Silas, Marisol, and many others—stood together on an improvised stage. Their manifesto, now a symbol of hope and defiance, was projected onto the sides of nearby buildings in bold, rebellious script.

In a voice that cut through the cacophony of the assembled crowd, Mara proclaimed, "Today, we celebrate not the absence of fear, but the courage to confront it. Today, we declare that our imperfections are not stains on our character—they are the brushstrokes of our true selves. And it is only by embracing the dark, unpredictable side of life that we can forge a future that is both genuine and revolutionary." The crowd roared in response, a sea of voices united in their shared belief that the time for change was now.

That night, as the rebels dispersed and the echoes of their rally faded into the urban night, Luminex was forever changed. The seeds of risk, sown with audacity and nurtured by the unyielding spirit of defiance, had blossomed into a revolution—a revolution that would continue to challenge the sterile dogmas of the old world and illuminate the path toward a future built on the raw, unfiltered beauty of imperfection.

And so, as the city's neon glow shimmered against the dark sky, every rebellious act, every risk taken in the name of authenticity, became a permanent part of Luminex's evolving narrative—a narrative that declared, with unrelenting sarcasm and defiant hope, that the only way forward was to risk it all. For in the relentless embrace of the dark, in the celebration of every flawed moment, lay the promise of innovation, transformation, and a future where vice was not condemned, but celebrated as the true catalyst of change.

CHAPTER SIX

Breaking the Chains of Conformity

In the heart of Luminex, beneath the sterile veneer of corporate towers and meticulously manicured boulevards, there simmered a quiet, seething fury. The city's well-oiled machinery of conformity churned on, its gears greased by the complacency of those who had long accepted the status quo as the only way to live. Yet, even amid the façade of order, there were cracks—small, almost imperceptible fissures through which the raw, untamed spirit of rebellion seeped. It was in these fissures that a new movement was beginning to form: a movement determined to shatter the chains of conformity that had kept the citizens of Luminex imprisoned in a gilded cage of mediocrity.

It began in whispers and furtive glances exchanged in the shadows of the city's busiest intersections. The everyday routine of beige-suited office workers, their lives mapped out in dull spreadsheets and tedious meetings, was slowly being questioned. For every automated nod in an elevator and every empty smile in a crowded subway, there was a spark of dissent—a moment when someone dared to wonder, "Is this really all there is?" And in those stolen moments, the first seeds of revolution were planted.

Among the first to notice these seeds was Lena—a mid-level manager in a drab, soulless corporation that prided itself on efficiency and predictability. Lena had once reveled in the security that conformity promised, the neat little boxes into which she was expected to file her thoughts and actions. But over time, the relentless hum of routine began to gnaw at her, until the perfection everyone else seemed so willing to tolerate appeared to her as nothing more than a prison. One cold, grey morning, as she sat in a sterile boardroom listening to another rehearsed presentation about quarterly targets, Lena's mind wandered. Instead of the usual nods and murmurs of agreement, she felt a prickling awareness—a call to something more authentic, something dangerous. In that moment, the chains that had bound her began to feel heavy and cumbersome, and she silently vowed that she would one day break free.

Her awakening, however, was not an isolated phenomenon. Across the city, in coffee shops, on crowded sidewalks, and in the dark recesses of forgotten alleyways, others were beginning to question the value of a life dictated by rigid norms. In one such quiet rebellion, a group of disenchanted souls began to meet in secret—a motley gathering that called itself "The Unbound." They met in a long-abandoned warehouse, its walls scarred by time and its air thick with the scent of must and possibility. Here, free from the prying eyes of a society that demanded uniformity, they dared to share their hidden truths, their messy failures, and the defiant hope that came from daring to be different.

At one of these clandestine meetings, the atmosphere was electric with the tension of suppressed desires and unspoken dreams. The room was lit by the soft glow of mismatched lamps and the occasional flicker of neon light filtering through broken windows. In a circle of mismatched chairs and salvaged tables, voices rose in a medley of confessions and declarations. There was Marcus, a former academic who had once preached the virtues of rationality but now saw the soul-crushing monotony of structured thought as a betrayal of creativity. There was also Jessa, a street artist whose bold, graffiti-covered murals had earned her a reputation as a renegade icon, and who now argued that conformity was the enemy of true artistic expression. And then there was Lena, who, having found the courage to question the life she once embraced, sat silently as the others spoke, her eyes reflecting both sorrow and fierce determination.

Marcus, his voice low and laced with irony, summed up the mood of the gathering: "We are told that stability is our salvation, that predictability is the bedrock of progress. Yet what do we gain from a life devoid of risk—a life in which every thought, every action, is pre-approved by some faceless authority? In our pursuit of order, we have traded our spontaneity, our passions, our very souls for a veneer of safety. And I say, no more." His words were met with murmurs of agreement, punctuated by the rustle of paper and the clinking of mismatched cups filled with bitter coffee.

Jessa, her eyes alight with defiant fire, leaned forward and continued, "Look around you—our city is a monument to conformity, a monument to the idea that being like everyone else is somehow virtuous. But what is virtue when it is demanded, when it is enforced, when it stifles the very essence of who we are? True virtue lies in our imperfections, in our scars, in our willingness to break the rules that bind us." Her tone was both mocking and sincere, a blend of sarcasm and genuine passion that sent a ripple of energy through the room.

Lena, though initially quiet, found herself drawn into the conversation. "I used to believe," she began hesitantly, "that following the rules was the safest way to live. But now I see that safety is an illusion—a gilded cage that keeps us from experiencing life in all its chaotic glory. I'm tired of being told that my ideas are too risky, that my failures are unacceptable. I want to break free from this prison of perfection, to live without fear of judgment." Her admission, raw and unfiltered, struck a chord with everyone present. In that vulnerable moment, the chains of conformity seemed to shatter, replaced by a collective resolve to reclaim their true selves.

As the meeting wore on, the conversation shifted from individual grievances to a broader discussion of strategy—a plan to dismantle the oppressive structures that had long dictated every facet of life in Luminex. The rebels of The Unbound agreed that breaking the chains of conformity required more than just private conversations and clandestine meetings. It demanded a public reckoning—a series of deliberate, high-impact actions that would force the old order to confront the undeniable truth of human diversity and creativity.

Marcus proposed a series of "Disruption Days," events where ordinary citizens would be encouraged to defy the norms of their daily lives. "Imagine a day when every person in the city is invited to do something radically different—wear outrageous colours to work, take a spontaneous detour on their commute, or simply speak their mind without fear of reprisal. For one day, let's see what happens when conformity is thrown out the window." His idea was met with both enthusiasm and cautious optimism. Some worried about the potential backlash from authorities, while others revealed in the thought of a collective uprising of individuality.

Jessa suggested that art be used as the spearhead of this rebellion. "Our murals, our installations, our performances—these are the tools we have to shake people out of their slumber," she declared. "We'll cover our city in art that challenges the notion of normalcy—a visual assault that reminds everyone that life is messy, unpredictable, and beautiful in its chaos." Her vision was one of a city transformed overnight, where every wall, every street corner, became a canvas for the celebration of imperfection.

Lena, now emboldened by the support of her newfound comrades, spoke of the power of storytelling. "Our lives," she said, "are full of stories that the mainstream would rather forget—stories of failure, of rebellion, of unexpected triumph. We need to tell those stories, to broadcast the truth that lies in our shared human experience. Through podcasts, zines, digital platforms—any means necessary—we can create a narrative that rejects the sanitised version of reality and embraces the wild, unfiltered truth." Her words resonated deeply, as many in the group had felt the suffocating pressure of being forced to wear masks of perfection in their professional and personal lives.

As the meeting drew to a close, a palpable sense of purpose filled the room. The rebels of The Unbound, once disparate individuals united only by a vague sense of discontent, now coalesced into a force with a clear vision: to break the chains of conformity that had long imprisoned the citizens of Luminex. They knew that the battle ahead would be arduous, that the powers that be would fight tooth and nail to preserve their immaculate order. But in their hearts burned the fierce conviction that true progress could only emerge when the sterile, oppressive norms of society were cast aside, replaced by the unpredictable, vibrant tapestry of genuine human expression.

Stepping out of the abandoned warehouse into the cool night air, Lena felt an unfamiliar lightness in her step—a sensation born from the unshackling of long-held fears. The city, with its rigid routines and meticulously maintained facades, loomed around her like a challenge. Every neon sign and every meticulously manicured garden was now a target for transformation—a reminder that conformity was not an immutable law of nature, but a man-made construct, ripe for dismantling.

On the streets of Luminex, the first acts of rebellion were already underway. Groups of people, inspired by the clandestine meetings of The Unbound, began to alter their routines in small, yet meaningful ways. In office corridors, whispers of “Disruption Day” spread like wildfire. A middle-aged accountant, emboldened by a newfound desire for authenticity, decided to swap his customary grey suit for a garish, mismatched ensemble that made heads turn and raised eyebrows. On the sidewalks, commuters took unexpected detours, choosing to walk through neighbourhoods they’d never seen, their paths marked by curiosity rather than habit. Even in the controlled environment of a corporate cafeteria, employees dared to engage in conversations about art, failure, and the meaning of true freedom—topics that had long been relegated to the fringes of polite society.

As Lena navigated these transformed streets, she felt herself becoming part of something larger than her individual awakening.

It was as if the collective energy of thousands of small acts of defiance was converging into a single, unstoppable force—a force that would eventually upend the entire system of conformity that had held Luminex in its grip for so long.

Meanwhile, back at the warehouse, The Unbound began to organise their next steps. They drafted preliminary plans for a city-wide "Day of Divergence," a coordinated effort to celebrate and amplify the beauty of individual expression. The blueprint was simple yet audacious: for one day, every citizen would be invited—no, compelled—to step out of the rigid molds that defined their existence and embrace the chaos of true freedom. Flyers were designed, digital campaigns were planned, and underground networks were set in motion to spread the word. The manifesto of The Unbound, which had started as whispered ideas in the dark, was now evolving into a full-fledged call to arms—a declaration that breaking the chains of conformity was not just a personal act, but a collective responsibility.

In the following days, anticipation rippled through the undercurrents of Luminex. People began to share their stories of rebellion on secret forums and through hastily printed zines. Social media, once dominated by curated images of perfection, was gradually being infiltrated by raw, unfiltered content—a montage of mismatched outfits, candid confessions of failure, and spontaneous celebrations of chaos. The digital landscape became a mirror of the physical one, a space where the collective yearning for authenticity could flourish without fear of censorship.

As night fell once more over Luminex, the atmosphere was charged with a sense of impending transformation. The rebels of The Unbound dispersed into the city's labyrinthine streets, each carrying with them the promise of change. Lena, her heart buoyed by the echoes of the warehouse meeting, stepped out onto a rain-slicked sidewalk, her mind alight with the possibilities of tomorrow. The chains of conformity, she realised, were not invincible—they were made of brittle assumptions and outdated fears, and with every act of rebellion, they were slowly being shattered.

The city, ever the paradoxical stage upon which these dramas unfolded, seemed to pulse with a hidden vitality—a silent acknowledgment that beneath the polished surface of order, something wild and untamed was awakening. In the flickering glow of streetlights and the reflective puddles on cracked pavement, the seeds of dissent took root. And as Lena walked on, she couldn't help but smile at the irony: a world that had once worshipped conformity was now, piece by piece, being reimagined by those brave enough to break free.

In this early chapter of the revolution, the battle against conformity was not waged with grand gestures or violent upheavals, but in the quiet, persistent acts of everyday defiance. It was in the small rebellions—a worker choosing a mismatched outfit, a student refusing to recite the approved version of history, a passerby pausing to admire a subversive mural—that the true nature of progress was revealed. Every act of individuality was a strike against the oppressive forces that sought to standardise every thought, every behaviour, every dream.

Thus, as the night deepened and the rebels scattered into the sprawling urban expanse of Luminex, the promise of a new era loomed on the horizon. A future where chains of conformity would be broken, where the raw, unpolished truth of human existence was celebrated, and where every soul was free to paint its own destiny without the oppressive brush of uniformity. And in that promise lay the undeniable truth that the revolution had only just begun.

The day after the clandestine warehouse meeting, the city of Luminex stirred with a restless energy that was both subtle and insidious. In the early light of dawn, as the concrete jungle slowly awakened to its monotonous routines, the seeds of rebellion—sown in whispered promises and secret gatherings—began to sprout in unexpected ways. The Unbound had sparked a quiet uprising, and now the movement was steadily gathering momentum, its influence creeping into the everyday lives of the people who had long traded authenticity for the security of conformity.

Lena, fresh from that transformative meeting, found herself navigating the gray corridors of her once-sterile workplace with an entirely new perspective. Every routine glance at the familiar beige walls and precisely arranged desks now set her teeth on edge. The office, with its relentless hum of printers and recycled motivational posters, had always been a symbol of order and control. But now it appeared to her as a prison designed to crush creativity. As she sat through another endless meeting—one where every comment was pre-approved and every idea sanitised—Lena's mind drifted to the whispered promises of The Unbound. In her quiet rebellion, she began jotting down small acts of defiance: a doodle on a memo pad here, a subtly altered email signature there. Each small subversion was a declaration of independence, a tiny fissure in the monolithic wall of conformity that surrounded her.

Meanwhile, far from the suffocating fluorescence of corporate cubicles, the movement was gathering steam in the city's neglected corners. In a forgotten café tucked away on a side street, a motley group of individuals—students, janitors, retirees, and even a few disillusioned executives—sat huddled around battered tables. They discussed everything from the latest underground art installations to the radical "Day of Divergence" that had been secretly circulating on social media channels. The idea was audacious: for one day, everyone in Luminex would be encouraged to cast off the chains of convention and live as authentically as possible, even if only for a few fleeting hours. The prospect of shaking off decades of ingrained routine lit a spark in even the most jaded souls. In hushed, conspiratorial tones, they debated how best to disrupt the status quo without inciting immediate, violent retribution from the omnipresent forces of authority.

At one table, a middle-aged man named Robert—a quiet accountant by day and a secret poet by night—leaned forward, his eyes bright with a mixture of fear and exhilaration. "I've spent my entire life crunching numbers for a company that worships efficiency above all else," he murmured, voice low enough for only his tablemates to hear. "And every day, I watch as my soul withers under the weight of someone else's rules. But what if, just for one day, we could all reject that? What if we could show the world that life isn't meant to be a sterile spreadsheet?" His words, laced with a bitter humour born of long-standing disillusionment, resonated with those around him. They saw in his eyes the reflection of their own hidden frustrations—a silent vow to reclaim the vibrancy that had been slowly drained from their lives.

Not far from that café, in a repurposed art studio that had become an unofficial hub for The Unbound, Jessa was hard at work. Her latest mural, a sprawling composition that spanned an entire side wall of an old warehouse, was nearing completion. The piece was a riotous explosion of colour and form—a direct challenge to the muted palettes of corporate propaganda that adorned so many of Luminex's sterile facades. In her work, Jessa depicted a chaotic human figure breaking free from chains that glistened like cold, unfeeling metal. "This," she whispered to a small group of onlookers gathered to admire her work, "is not just art—it's a statement. Every stroke of my brush is a middle finger to a world that insists on uniformity. It's a celebration of our scars, our messy, unpredictable humanity." Her tone dripped with the kind of raw, sarcastic passion that had become the hallmark of the rebellion. Those present could see in her art and her words a tangible embodiment of the desire to break free from the oppressive chains that had held them captive for so long.

Across the city, the digital battleground was heating up as well. Silas and Marisol's underground platform, a raw and unfiltered haven for dissent, had begun to attract a steadily growing audience. The platform was an uncurated stream of unedited truth—a counter-narrative to the pristine, overproduced content churned out by mainstream media. Here, anyone brave enough to share their unvarnished thoughts, no matter how messy or controversial, could find an audience. Late at night, when the city's more diligent censors had long since powered down their surveillance systems, the digital rebels would gather virtually to share their experiences of living under the crushing weight of conformity. Heated debates, bitter confessions, and brilliant bursts of creativity flowed like digital graffiti across the screen. "We're not here to play it safe," one user typed in a stream of raw text, "we're here to tear down the walls of this sanitised prison, one unscripted moment at a time." The sentiment resonated deeply with the digital denizens, whose collective voice was growing louder with every passing day.

Amidst this swelling tide of rebellion, the organizers of the "Day of Divergence" finalized their plans. Flyers, printed on recycled paper and scrawled with vivid, rebellious fonts, began to appear on telephone poles, in bus shelters, and even taped to the windshields of government vehicles. The message was simple and unyielding: for one day, cast off your masks, break your routines, and embrace the chaos of true freedom. The plan was to orchestrate a city-wide disruption—a cascade of small, spontaneous acts of individuality that would ripple outward until even the most entrenched bastions of conformity could no longer ignore the call. The organizers knew that such a day would be fraught with risks, that the powers that be would respond with all the force of an institution desperate to maintain its grip. But they also knew that the potential rewards—a collective awakening, a resurgence of authentic human expression—were worth every ounce of risk.

In a secret meeting held in the back room of an inconspicuous laundromat, Lena and a few of her colleagues from The Unbound gathered to discuss the logistics. Over the hum of washing machines and the clatter of spinning dryers, they hashed out the finer details of their plan. "We need to make this a true, unfiltered experience," Lena insisted, her tone fervent and determined. "This isn't about one-off acts of rebellion. It's about creating an environment where everyone can feel the thrill of being different—where conformity is not a default state but a choice we consciously reject." Her colleagues, a mix of disgruntled office workers, rebellious creatives, and a few disillusioned managers, nodded in agreement. They shared stories of days spent in endless, mind-numbing routine, and of nights spent dreaming of a life that allowed them to express the full spectrum of their humanity, no matter how messy or unpredictable.

One of the group, a soft-spoken woman named Anita, recalled a moment of quiet defiance that had transformed her perspective. "I used to believe that the only safe way to live was to follow the rules," she said, her voice trembling slightly with emotion. "But one day, I wore a scarf that wasn't part of the approved color palette to a meeting, and instead of being reprimanded, I felt an overwhelming sense of liberation. It was as if, in that small act of disobedience, I had reclaimed a piece of myself that had been lost to the monotony of perfection. That moment changed me." Her words, gentle yet piercing, served as a reminder that even the smallest deviations from the norm could spark a profound internal revolution.

As the plans for the Day of Divergence solidified, the rebels prepared for the inevitable backlash. The authorities, sensing the growing undercurrent of unrest, began to tighten their grip on public spaces. Surveillance cameras were repositioned, and a new wave of "safety measures" was announced on local news channels with all the sterile bravado of bureaucratic propaganda. Yet, the more the state clamored for order, the more the citizens of Luminex began to see the irony in their constant plea for conformity. In the calculated smiles of government officials and the carefully rehearsed public statements, a bitter humor was discernible—a silent acknowledgment that, in a world where everything was forced to be perfect, imperfection was the only authentic rebellion.

Throughout the city, acts of subtle defiance began to ripple outward. In a sleek, glass-encased office building, a janitor, tired of the endless cycle of monotony, decided to leave behind a single, carefully placed sticker on a polished door that read, "Break Free." In a crowded subway car, a teenager in a faded hoodie boldly wore a T-shirt emblazoned with the words "Unbound" in clashing, defiant colors. Every small act was a silent, yet powerful, reminder that conformity was not the inevitable destiny of the people of Luminex.

The digital world, too, buzzed with anticipation. As the Day of Divergence drew nearer, the underground platform overflowed with user-generated content—raw images, unedited videos, candid testimonials of lives spent under the yoke of uniformity. Posts that were once whispered in hushed tones now roared with defiant vigor. The platform became a digital gallery of rebellion, where every contribution was a testament to the beauty of being unapologetically oneself.

One particular post that began circulating widely featured a collage of faces—diverse, unfiltered, and proudly imperfect. Accompanying the image was a caption that read, "In our differences, we find strength. In our imperfections, we find beauty. Conformity is a prison, but rebellion is freedom." The post quickly went viral among the digital denizens of Luminex, sparking countless conversations and inspiring many to question the sterile norms they had once accepted without thought.

By now, the Day of Divergence was set to be more than just a symbolic gesture—it was on the brink of becoming a catalyst for a new era. As night fell once more over the sprawling metropolis, the energy in Luminex was palpable. The city's familiar rhythms had been disrupted; the relentless march of conformity had begun to falter under the weight of its own tired expectations. In every street, every alley, every unnoticed corner, the promise of liberation shone like a rebellious spark waiting to ignite a blaze.

In the hours before the planned event, The Unbound continued their clandestine operations with a mixture of meticulous planning and raw, impulsive creativity. Lena, who had emerged as one of the movement's most vocal organizers, worked late into the night drafting emails, coordinating with like-minded individuals, and even slipping past security in the corridors of her former workplace to distribute small flyers. "Every whisper of dissent," she wrote in one carefully worded message, "is a seed that can grow into a tree of change. Don't be afraid to let your true self shine—even if it means standing out like a scar on a perfectly smooth surface." Her words were both an invitation and a challenge, a call to arms for those who had long been silenced by the demands of conformity.

As midnight approached and the city was bathed in the ghostly glow of streetlights and neon, the rebels of Luminex dispersed into the urban night. Their hearts beat with a mixture of apprehension and excitement, each one aware that the coming day could change everything. In the quiet before dawn, while the forces of the old order lay in wait with their surveillance and restrictive policies, the people of Luminex were on the cusp of reclaiming their individuality. The Day of Divergence was no longer a mere idea—it was a promise that every small act of defiance, every deliberate moment of authenticity, would shatter the chains of conformity and open a path to a future where every soul was free to be imperfect.

And so, as the first light of dawn began to break over the horizon, casting long shadows over the city's sterile facades, the stage was set. In the cool, tentative light of a new day, the people of Luminex would soon awaken to a world that no longer demanded their compliance. Instead, it would celebrate the wild, unrestrained, and beautiful chaos of their true selves. The Day of Divergence was near, and with it, the promise of breaking the chains that had bound them for far too long.

Dawn broke over Luminex with the reluctant promise of change—a pale, almost mocking light that crept over the city's sterile facades and exposed the deep-seated fissures of conformity. In the early hours of the long-anticipated Day of Divergence, the streets were an eerie blend of anticipation and quiet rebellion. The familiar drone of early traffic was punctuated by the soft murmur of dissent, as if every citizen, from the high-rise office worker to the solitary street artist, had woken with a secret: today, the chains would begin to break.

Lena stepped out into this uncertain morning with a newfound determination that vibrated in every step. The cold air bit at her cheeks, a reminder that freedom was never free—but that was a cost she was willing to pay. As she walked along the sidewalks, she noticed subtle transformations everywhere. A group of young professionals, once indistinguishable in their matching suits, now strolled together in outfits of deliberately mismatched colors, their eyes alight with the thrill of defiance. A poster, hastily torn from a lamppost, proclaimed in bold, anarchic letters: "Normalcy is a Lie."

Even the stern-faced security guards at a sleek corporate building couldn't hide a fleeting look of uncertainty as they passed a newly painted mural that splattered chaotic imagery across the once-pristine wall.

In a modest apartment that overlooked a busy avenue, Marcus, one of the early voices from The Unbound, sat at a cluttered desk, feverishly typing his thoughts onto an old laptop. His document—half manifesto, half personal diary—was filled with reflections on the oppressive normalcy he had spent years enduring. "Today," he wrote in jagged, urgent prose, "we dismantle the expectations that have held us prisoner. We embrace our quirks, our mistakes, and even our failures, for it is in our very imperfection that we discover the raw truth of life." His words, imbued with a dark humor and defiant sincerity, were soon echoed across digital channels as his post went viral on the underground platform.

Meanwhile, in the heart of a bustling café that had become an unofficial meeting spot for dissenters, a motley crew gathered over coffee that was as bitter as the truths they shared. Robert, the quiet accountant-poet, recited a new piece he had penned just moments before:

"Today we shatter the mirror of conformity,
each crack a testament to our reclaimed souls."

His voice, soft yet trembling with conviction, sent ripples through the table. Around him, conversations buzzed about dreams deferred and the exhilarating terror of finally stepping off the well-worn path. Even the regulars—those who had once considered such conversations the ramblings of radicals—now found themselves nodding in reluctant agreement. There was an energy in the air, a palpable sense that the status quo was on the verge of being upended.

At the designated hub for the Day of Divergence—a long-abandoned subway station that had been transformed overnight into a pop-up festival of rebellion—dozens of citizens converged. The station, once echoing with the predictable clatter of commuters, now throbbed with the pulsating beat of underground music, raw street art, and the vibrant chatter of liberated souls. Banners fluttered from the crumbling ceilings, their slogans a collage of defiant messages: “Dare to Diverge,” “Embrace Your Flaws,” and “Conformity Kills Creativity.”

Lena found herself amid this chaotic celebration, heart pounding as she took in the sight of ordinary people boldly rejecting their prescribed roles. In one corner, a group of office workers had transformed their mundane lunch break into a spontaneous dance-off, their laughter ringing out as a direct challenge to the oppressive monotony of corporate life. In another, a lone woman had set up a makeshift stage where she recited verses that deconstructed the sanitised narratives of success, her voice trembling with both anger and hope.

Across the vast, graffiti-lined walls of the station, Jessa’s latest mural—an explosive amalgam of color and raw emotion—dominated a once-forgotten wall. The artwork depicted a human figure, limbs outstretched in defiance, shattering a set of cold, metallic chains that once bound it. “These chains,” the accompanying text read in jagged script, “are built not of iron but of our own resignation. Break them, and become who you were meant to be.” The sight stirred something deep within those who gazed upon it—a flicker of recognition, a spark of courage.

Amid the crowd, Silas and Marisol manned a small booth where they demonstrated the digital platform they had built—a space where voices unfiltered by corporate algorithms could converge and ignite further acts of rebellion. The booth was modest, set up on a makeshift table, yet it drew an unexpected surge of interest. Young tech enthusiasts, curious artists, and even a few hardened professionals took turns exploring its features. Each interaction was met with knowing smiles and murmurs of approval. “This is where the real conversation happens,” one user whispered as they scrolled through a live feed of unedited thoughts and raw creative bursts from across the city. The platform was a digital haven—a chaotic tapestry of uncurated truth that stood in stark contrast to the glossy, manipulated feeds of the mainstream.

As the morning unfolded, the Day of Divergence began to assert itself more boldly. In a series of coordinated flash mobs, groups of citizens executed their planned acts of individuality. In front of a towering bank building, a contingent of students performed an impromptu skit that parodied the rigid protocols of corporate life—mocking the sterile lingo and rehearsed gestures of the establishment. Their performance, filled with biting sarcasm and anarchic humor, drew cheers and even a few stunned smiles from passersby. It was a performance that laid bare the absurdity of a society that demanded uniformity, showing that true freedom lay in the spontaneous, unpredictable moments of living.

Elsewhere, on a busy thoroughfare lined with sleek storefronts, an elderly tailor—long resigned to a life of quiet conformity—stopped his daily routine to set up an impromptu exhibition of his own designs. His garments, crafted with intricate detail and wild, unorthodox patterns, were a direct rebuke to the monotonous uniforms that had once defined his world. "These are my true creations," he declared in a voice that trembled with both pride and defiance, "woven from the threads of my own experiences, not the dull prescriptions of a world that values sameness over substance." His display, though modest, became a beacon for those who had always felt out of place in a society that prized homogeneity.

At the heart of these myriad acts of rebellion, Lena wandered the transformed streets, absorbing the sights and sounds of a city in flux. With every step, she encountered evidence that the oppressive chains of conformity were beginning to fracture. A mural on a once-pristine wall declared, "Normal is the New Insane," its letters jagged and defiant against the backdrop of a corporate skyline. In a small park, a group of teenagers, their hair dyed in vibrant hues and clothes splattered with DIY patches, held an impromptu debate about the meaning of true freedom. Their voices, youthful and fierce, clashed and harmonized in a symphony of ideas that defied the bland narratives of the past.

Yet amid the exhilaration, there was an undercurrent of tension—a silent, collective awareness that the forces of conformity were not oblivious to these transformations. Rumors had begun to circulate of increased patrols by security forces, of more cameras being installed on street corners, and of whispered orders from high up in the bureaucratic hierarchy to "restore order" at all costs. But for the rebels, these threats only added to the thrill. Risk was the very lifeblood of their movement, and each potential setback was seen as an opportunity to demonstrate their unwavering resolve. "They may try to tighten their grip," Lena thought as she passed a patrol car with blinking red lights, "but the more they push, the more we push back."

In the midst of this charged atmosphere, a central hub of the rebellion emerged—a repurposed community center that had become the nerve center for planning, organizing, and celebrating every act of defiance. Here, the leaders of The Unbound convened once more. The air was thick with the aroma of strong coffee, the sound of fervent conversation, and the low hum of digital devices streaming live updates from the streets. It was a place where the raw passion of the revolution was distilled into plans and strategies. Maps of the city were spread out on tables, marked with the locations of recent acts of rebellion and potential targets for future interventions. The room buzzed with energy as each member contributed ideas, debated tactics, and shared stories of personal triumph over the suffocating monotony of conformity.

At one table, a group of young activists discussed the significance of collective action. "Our strength isn't just in the individual acts," one of them declared, his voice earnest and defiant, "it's in how those acts come together to create a tidal wave of change. Every sticker, every mural, every bold step out of your comfort zone—each one is a spark. And together, those sparks will ignite a conflagration that even the highest towers of conformity cannot withstand." The sentiment was met with nods and murmurs of agreement—a chorus of voices united by a shared vision of a future that celebrated difference and individuality.

Meanwhile, on a quiet corner of the community center, Silas and Marisol huddled over a laptop, their faces illuminated by the flickering screen. They were tracking the digital pulse of the rebellion—a sprawling network of posts, videos, and messages that captured the raw, unedited truth of what was unfolding in Luminex. "Look at this," Silas murmured, pointing to a series of images showing unexpected acts of defiance on corporate billboards and public transit. "This is the sound of change—the chaos of a society finally waking up." Marisol nodded, her fingers dancing over the keys as she integrated new features into their platform, determined to ensure that every dissenting voice could be heard.

As the morning wore on, the momentum of the Day of Divergence swelled to a fever pitch. The digital and physical realms converged into a singular, vibrant display of resistance. With every passing minute, the actions of ordinary citizens—each a small, deliberate break from the chains of conformity—wove themselves into the larger tapestry of the rebellion. And as Lena continued to navigate the transformed cityscape, her heart beat with the steady rhythm of hope and defiance. In each glance exchanged between strangers, in every whispered conversation about dreams long suppressed, she saw the promise of a future that was as unpredictable as it was free.

The city itself, with its towering glass and steel monuments to a bygone era of sterile perfection, seemed to tremble beneath the force of this collective uprising. The very streets, once immaculate and meticulously controlled, now bore the unmistakable signs of transformation: splashes of color where monotony once reigned, voices raised in defiant protest against a world that had long celebrated conformity. Every act of individuality—no matter how small—was a declaration that the time for quiet submission was over. The chains that had bound Luminex for so long were beginning to break, one rebellious act at a time.

As the Day of Divergence continued its relentless march, the rebels of The Unbound felt a profound shift within themselves. They were no longer merely a group of disaffected souls gathering in hidden corners; they had become the architects of a new narrative, one where the freedom to be imperfect was not a privilege but a right. In that awakening, there was both joy and sorrow—a bittersweet recognition that with every chain broken, a part of the old self was forever lost, replaced by a fierce, unyielding commitment to authenticity.

By midday, the city was a living, breathing testament to this transformation. In corporate boardrooms that once echoed with sterile applause, whispered conversations of rebellion now trickled in—small cracks in the façade of obedience. At busy intersections, impromptu debates about art, freedom, and individuality replaced the mindless recitation of rote schedules. And in every public space, the mark of the rebellion was visible: a patchwork of slogans, graffiti, and art installations that boldly declared that conformity was no longer the norm.

As Lena joined a group of coworkers on their lunch break—a motley collection of individuals who had also begun to reject the tiresome dictates of corporate life—she felt a collective pulse of resistance. Over hurried bites of food and stolen moments of conversation, they shared their newfound perspectives, each one affirming that the day's rebellion was only the beginning of something much larger. In the midst of their quiet conversations, the fear of retaliation was overshadowed by a powerful, shared desire for change—a desire that had been kindled in the dark corners of The Unbound and was now blazing across the city.

In that powerful moment of unity, as the sun cast long shadows over a city in revolt, Lena realized that breaking the chains of conformity was not an isolated act of rebellion but a revolution of the spirit. Each person who dared to be different, who challenged the imposed uniformity of their existence, contributed to a mosaic of change—a mosaic that, when viewed as a whole, painted a picture of a world reborn in its own beautiful imperfection.

And so, as the Day of Divergence carried on with unabated intensity, the movement that had begun in whispered meetings and quiet acts of defiance now roared like an unstoppable tide.

Every mural, every daring act, every voice raised in rebellion was a step toward a future where conformity would no longer dictate the terms of existence. In that future, every soul was free to celebrate its unique chaos, every imperfection a mark of honour, every risk taken a stride toward a truth that was raw, unfiltered, and unequivocally real.

In the urban symphony of dissent that echoed throughout Luminex, the promise of breaking the chains of conformity was no longer a distant dream—it was an imminent reality, forged by the collective will of those who dared to defy. And in that pulsating heart of the rebellion, as the city transformed under the weight of its own awakening, a new chapter of freedom was being written—one that would forever alter the landscape of a society that had long prized sameness over the unpredictable beauty of individuality.

As dusk settled over Luminex and the Day of Divergence reached its fevered apex, the city's dark underbelly became the arena for a battle of wills. The authorities, roused by the escalating acts of rebellion, began to flex their repressive muscle with a precision that was both chilling and ironically predictable. Surveillance vans, their windows darkened and tires hissing against rain-slicked asphalt, patrolled the streets with renewed urgency. In government offices, executives huddled over reports that painted a grim picture of disorder—a disorder that the state was determined to stamp out with all the force of bureaucratic might.

On the very same streets where yesterday's spontaneous celebrations had danced in defiant colors, the air now buzzed with an uneasy tension. Every spray-painted slogan and every liberated mural was now under sharper scrutiny. The state's response was swift and ruthless: permits for public gatherings were suddenly revoked, and a wave of "public order" initiatives was launched. Ironically, the more the government tried to restore its cherished order, the more its actions confirmed what the rebels had long claimed—that the perfection they preached was nothing but an elaborate sham.

In a stark, windowless command center deep within a nondescript government building, a cadre of officials gathered around a polished conference table. Their faces were set in grim lines as they reviewed footage from hundreds of surveillance cameras scattered across the city. One senior officer, his voice clipped and emotionless, announced, "We have documented numerous instances of unauthorized gatherings, unsanctioned public art, and blatant disruptions of the established routine. We must act decisively." His words, delivered with all the sterile confidence of a man whose life was dedicated to order, were met with silent nods. Plans were quickly set in motion—targeted raids, increased patrols, and the deployment of digital tracking measures meant to root out the source of the dissent. It was a calculated counteroffensive, one designed to remind the citizens of Luminex that while their voices might rise in rebellion, the state's power was absolute.

Yet even as the machinery of repression churned to life, the spirit of The Unbound refused to be silenced. In a nondescript, repurposed industrial space that had become the nerve center for the rebellion, Lena and her comrades gathered once again. The atmosphere was charged with a mix of adrenaline and grim determination. Maps of the city were spread across scarred tables, annotated with the latest reports of clashes, flash mobs, and covert interventions. Digital feeds from Silas and Marisol's underground platform continued to stream in real time, their raw, unfiltered content now more critical than ever.

Lena's eyes, once weary from the drudgery of corporate life, now burned with a fervour fueled by the certainty that the struggle for authenticity was far from over. "They want to show us that we must be docile, that our defiance is dangerous," she said in a low, measured tone, addressing the small circle of rebels gathered before her. "But every action they take to impose order only validates our cause. They tighten their grip, and we slip through their fingers." Her words were met with murmurs of agreement and a few determined nods. It was clear that the rebels were not naïve; they understood that the forces of conformity would not yield without a fight. Instead, each new measure of repression was seen as an opportunity—a challenge to be met with creativity and relentless resolve.

Marcus, whose quiet wisdom had already inspired countless acts of defiance, leaned over the maps and pointed to a series of red dots—locations of recent state crackdowns. "Look here," he said, his voice tinged with both bitterness and resolve, "this is where they've tried to stifle us. But every time they strike, we adapt. Last week's raid on the Central Square only made people even more determined to gather on their own terms. Our digital channels are lighting up with reports of the crackdown, and that exposure is our ammunition." His words resonated deeply with the group. They were no longer fighting abstract battles; they were engaged in a concrete war—a war waged on both the physical streets and the digital networks that connected every rebel in the city.

In another corner of the room, Jessa, her hands still stained with the remnants of fresh spray paint, recounted how her latest mural—an explosive portrait of a faceless bureaucrat dissolving into a burst of chaotic color—had been defaced within hours of its unveiling. "They couldn't let it stand," she said with a bitter laugh, her tone laced with sardonic humor. "They had to scrub away our art, our truth. But in doing so, they only made it more powerful. Now, that image is shared across social media as a symbol of resistance—a reminder that even if they try to erase us, we'll keep coming back, bolder and louder." Her defiant optimism lit a spark in those around her, affirming that every attempt to silence the rebellion only amplified its message.

Outside the command center, the city itself writhed under the weight of conflicting forces. In one neighborhood, an impromptu blockade of protestors had formed near a government building, their chants and slogans echoing down the street. Amid the chaos, a small contingent of uniformed officers advanced with determined precision, their faces set in grim masks of authority. But as they neared, the protestors—armed not with weapons but with nothing more than their voices and a fierce desire for change—raised their hands in defiance, their chants transforming into a cacophony of demands for freedom. In that moment, the standoff became a microcosm of the larger struggle: a collision between a state desperate to maintain its sanitised order and a people unwilling to sacrifice their individuality at any cost.

Silas and Marisol, monitoring these events from the safety of their digital domain, exchanged a look that conveyed both concern and a steely determination. "This is just the beginning," Silas murmured, his eyes glued to the live feeds. "They think they can scare us into submission with cameras and uniformed threats, but every confrontation only proves that our resolve is unbreakable." Marisol, fingers poised over her keyboard, added, "Our platform is witnessing a surge. People are flooding it with stories, images, and raw accounts of what's happening on the streets. They're taking control of the narrative—and that, my friend, is the most powerful tool they have."

The digital revolution was in full swing. Across Luminex, ordinary citizens—once silent cogs in the machine of conformity—had taken to their devices to share their newfound voices. A video of a young woman defiantly reciting a poem about the beauty of chaos went viral, its stark message a rallying cry for those who had long felt trapped by the pressures of an immaculate society. Memes, hashtags, and viral posts flooded the underground platform, each one a digital kerfuffle that chipped away at the towering edifice of the old order. In this interconnected web of dissent, every shared story, every raw confession, and every act of courage was magnified, reverberating far beyond the confines of Luminex.

Back at the community center, as dusk approached once more and the rebels reconvened for an evening debrief, the mood was a curious mix of exhaustion and exhilaration. Lena addressed the group once again, her voice resonating with a measured passion born of hard-won battles. "Today, we've seen that the state's crackdown is not a sign of weakness—it's a sign of their desperation. They fear us because we are the embodiment of everything they wish to suppress. And every time they try to reassert their control, we prove that our spirit is unyielding." Her words hung in the air, a solemn promise that the fight was far from over.

The meeting shifted to tactical discussions. Plans were laid for the next phase of the rebellion—targeted actions designed not only to defy the state's restrictions but to actively dismantle the systems of conformity. Some proposed digital strikes against the propaganda channels of the authorities, while others suggested coordinated public demonstrations in key civic spaces. There was talk of launching a series of "Conformity Cracks"—a planned release of unfiltered stories and art across all available media channels, aimed at exposing the brittle underbelly of the sanitised order. Every idea, no matter how radical, was met with fervent debate and a shared understanding that the path to genuine freedom was paved with risk and relentless innovation.

As the night deepened, the atmosphere in the community center grew almost electric. The rebels knew that the coming days would be fraught with challenges—each act of defiance would be met with a countermeasure, each bold step would be shadowed by the risk of severe repercussions. Yet, in that moment, there was an undeniable clarity: the chains of conformity were cracking, and with each fissure, a new possibility emerged. The oppressive structures that had once dictated every thought, every behavior, every dream were beginning to crumble under the collective weight of unbridled individuality.

Outside, the city of Luminex lay in a state of uneasy truce. The uniformed patrols continued their relentless rounds, their headlights slicing through the darkness like accusatory eyes. But even as the state tightened its grip, the citizens—spurred on by the intoxicating allure of rebellion—found innovative ways to express their defiance. A small group of young activists, huddled in a deserted park, organized a midnight "Freedom Flash Mob" that saw them break into a choreographed dance of protest, their movements both playful and provocatively subversive. Every spontaneous act, every shared smile between rebels and ordinary citizens alike, was a defiant testament to the belief that conformity was not destiny, but an obstacle to be overcome.

In the shadowed corridors of Luminex's urban landscape, the narrative was being rewritten one defiant act at a time. The community center, the digital platform, and every street corner had become the battleground for a struggle that transcended the mere aesthetics of rebellion—it was a fight for the soul of the city. And while the authorities might marshal their forces and attempt to paint dissent as chaos and disorder, the rebels knew that true progress lay in the freedom to be imperfect, to be unpredictable, and above all, to be unapologetically human.

As the night drew to a close and the first hints of dawn crept over the horizon, the rebels dispersed into the labyrinthine streets once more. Their hearts, heavy with the weight of what had been achieved and the uncertainty of what lay ahead, beat in unison with the restless pulse of a city on the brink of transformation. Lena lingered for a moment on a rain-soaked street corner, watching as the neon glow faded into the pale light of morning. In that quiet, reflective pause, she allowed herself a rare smile—a recognition that in every crack of the oppressive wall, there was a sliver of light, a promise of freedom.

For in the breaking of the chains of conformity, every act of defiance—every unscripted moment of individuality—was a victory over the sterile, homogenized world that had long held them captive. And as Luminex prepared to face a new day, the rebels carried with them the unyielding belief that the spirit of divergence was not something that could be extinguished by force. It was a flame, fueled by the raw, unpredictable nature of the human soul—a flame that would continue to burn, even in the face of the darkest repression.

Night had fallen again over Luminex, a city that had become both battlefield and canvas in the struggle against sterile uniformity. In the aftermath of the Day of Divergence, the rebels had proven that the seeds of rebellion could sprout even in the most meticulously controlled environments. Now, in the quiet hours before the dawn of a new era, the movement—once a series of scattered, individual acts of defiance—had matured into a unified force poised to break the chains of conformity for good.

In the heart of a dilapidated district, where the glow of neon was tempered by the scars of urban decay, a final gathering of The Unbound took place in a long-abandoned community center. The building's walls, once faded and forgotten, were now adorned with vibrant slogans and rebellious murals—a patchwork of images that bore witness to the struggle for authenticity. Here, under the low hum of flickering fluorescent lights, the rebels convened for one last strategic session, aware that every moment was both a triumph and a challenge in their continuing fight.

Lena, whose transformation from a cog in the corporate machine to a fierce rebel leader had become an inspiration in itself, stood at the head of a makeshift stage. Her eyes, steely with determination and tempered by the hardships of relentless defiance, scanned the crowd of allies gathered before her. "Tonight," she began, her voice echoing in the cavernous space, "we solidify everything we've fought for. Every act of rebellion, every spark of individuality that has blossomed in the dark corners of this city, has led us to this moment." Her tone was both sardonic and resolute—a reminder that the oppressive structures they sought to dismantle were built on lies, and that every chain shattered was a victory for the human spirit.

Around her, the room pulsed with energy as the rebels reviewed the progress made over the past days. Maps scrawled with red dots marking state crackdowns, digital feeds displaying live images of unsanctioned protests, and hastily printed flyers with defiant messages all testified to a revolution that had infiltrated every level of society. Marcus, his face lined with both exhaustion and pride, pointed to a series of reports on a worn table. "Look at this," he said, his voice rough with emotion, "every attempt by the state to quash our movement has only amplified our message. Our art, our voices, our very existence have become a mirror reflecting their hypocrisy." His words were met with murmurs of agreement—a bittersweet acknowledgment that the more the authorities tried to enforce order, the louder the people's longing for freedom became.

Outside the community center, Luminex continued its uneasy metamorphosis. In the corporate district, executives huddled in sleek boardrooms, their faces masked in forced composure as they scrambled to devise countermeasures. Press releases spoke of "re-establishing civic order" and "upholding community values," yet every statement dripped with the sterile rhetoric of a system desperate to cling to its brittle power. The polished facades of glass towers, once symbols of untouchable control, now bore the subtle, yet unmistakable marks of subversion—a discreet sticker here, a spray-painted phrase there, evidence that even the most isolated bastions of conformity were not immune to the insidious spread of rebellion.

In a quiet residential block, an elderly couple—long accustomed to the monotony of their regulated lives—found themselves transfixed by an unexpected display of defiance. A mural, freshly created on the wall of their apartment building, depicted a burst of chaotic color and a solitary figure breaking free from a tangle of metallic chains. "They call it vandalism," the wife remarked with a wry smile as she clutched her husband's hand, "but to me, it's a declaration of life. A reminder that even in our twilight years, we're still capable of resisting." Her husband, nodding slowly, added, "Maybe it's time we remembered what it means to live." In that moment, the impact of the rebels' efforts transcended generational divides, touching even those who had long been resigned to the predictable rhythm of conformity.

Back at the community center, the rebels' discussion turned toward the next phase of their revolution—a plan to not only defend their gains but to push further into the corridors of power. Jessa, her hands still streaked with the residue of her latest mural masterpiece, spoke up with a fiery intensity. "We've shown them that our spirit is unbreakable," she declared, "but now we must take it further. Our art isn't just a reaction—it's a catalyst. It's a message that every time you try to silence us, you only make our voices louder." She proposed a series of coordinated public interventions—installations, flash mobs, and digital strikes designed to disrupt the sanitised order of the city on a grand scale. "We want to turn the very instruments of repression—those cameras, those screens, those boring announcements—against themselves. Let the state see what happens when it underestimates the power of the individual."

Silas, ever the quiet philosopher of the movement, added his perspective in a tone that was as measured as it was defiant. "Breaking the chains of conformity isn't just about small acts of rebellion," he said softly, "it's about creating a new paradigm. We need to dismantle the myth that order is synonymous with safety. The truth is, order can be a prison—a gilded cage that stifles the wild, unpredictable nature of our humanity. And if we can show that chaos, that beautiful, unruly chaos, is the source of true innovation, then we've already won half the battle." His words, laden with a mixture of melancholy and hope, resonated deeply with the younger activists who hung on every syllable.

Marisol, who had been quietly monitoring their digital channels throughout the day, now joined in with a keen sense of urgency. "Our platform is now a beacon," she explained, "a digital sanctuary where every unsanitised thought, every raw emotion, is amplified. We're not just fighting back—we're creating an alternative space for truth. And the more people join us there, the more difficult it will become for the state to ignore our existence." Her eyes shone with fierce determination as she outlined plans to expand the network further, ensuring that every corner of Luminex, both physical and virtual, would pulse with the rebellious spirit of the movement.

As the discussion continued, the room gradually quieted into a reflective pause—a moment of collective introspection before the final push of the evening. The rebels knew that the night ahead would not be without danger. The state's forces were still out there, lurking behind the veneer of order, ready to pounce on any sign of organized dissent. Yet in that vulnerability, there was a paradoxical strength. Each risk, each act of defiance, had already chipped away at the foundation of conformity. Every time the state tightened its grip, the people's yearning for freedom grew even stronger.

Outside, the wind picked up, carrying with it the faint sounds of a city in revolt—a symphony of protest, laughter, and unfiltered expression that defied the sterile cadence of everyday life. The once-quiet avenues were now alive with whispers of revolution, as every passerby, every hurried glance, seemed to carry the spark of individuality. The rebellion had moved beyond the confines of secret meetings and digital forums; it was now woven into the very fabric of Luminex, a mosaic of vibrant, defiant fragments that no amount of repression could ever fully erase.

In a final, unifying moment before the night's decisive actions commenced, Lena stepped out onto a rain-washed balcony that overlooked the sprawling cityscape. The view was a stark reminder of the divide between the towering, pristine monuments of power and the gritty, unapologetic chaos of the streets below. In that moment of solitary reflection, she allowed herself a brief, rueful smile—a mixture of dark humor and steely resolve. "They can try to build walls, they can try to impose order," she murmured to herself, "but they'll never understand that the human spirit is too wild, too unruly, to be caged." Her words, carried away by the chill wind, resonated like a promise—a promise that the revolution was not a fleeting burst of anger, but an enduring force that would continue to grow, evolve, and transform.

As the final minutes of the Day of Divergence ticked away, the community center became a hive of activity. Plans were being finalized, final instructions were whispered, and the air was thick with anticipation. The rebels were poised to launch a series of coordinated public interventions that would mark the next phase of their uprising—a phase designed not merely to resist, but to fundamentally reshape the narrative of Luminex. The details were meticulously laid out: a network of flash mobs to disrupt key intersections, digital campaigns to hijack state-controlled media, and art installations that would turn public spaces into living galleries of dissent.

The energy in the room was palpable—a convergence of fear, hope, and fierce determination that electrified every word and every gesture. In that charged atmosphere, it became clear that breaking the chains of conformity was more than an abstract ideal; it was a tangible, lived experience that each rebel carried in their heart. They had all tasted the bitter, exhilarating flavor of defiance and knew that no matter how hard the state tried to clamp down, the human desire for freedom was insatiable.

As midnight approached and the final preparations were made, the rebels dispersed once more into the darkened streets of Luminex. The city, now a sprawling canvas of audacious art and whispered rebellion, awaited the coming surge—a wave of public defiance that promised to dismantle the oppressive structures of conformity, one daring act at a time.

And so, on that fateful night, as the neon lights flickered defiantly against the starless sky, the chains of conformity began to crack and break, yielding to the relentless force of the human spirit. Every act of rebellion, every unscripted moment of individuality, reverberated like a defiant chorus—a chorus that declared, with dark sarcasm and unyielding passion, that the future belonged to those who dared to be different. In the shadow of the towering monuments of order, the people of Luminex were writing a new story—a story in which conformity was no longer a given, but a choice to be challenged and ultimately overcome.

As the first hints of dawn began to bleed into the night, the echoes of the rebellion surged through the city—a final, resounding affirmation that the chains had been shattered. In that triumphant moment, every rebel knew that while the battle was far from over, the revolution had already etched its mark on the soul of Luminex. And in the silent promise of that new day lay the unyielding truth: that in breaking the chains of conformity, they had reclaimed not only their freedom but the very essence of what it meant to be alive.

CHAPTER SEVEN

The Convergence: Where Vice Meets Virtue

Luminex had always been a city of extremes—where the seething undercurrents of vice clashed violently with the rigid façade of conventional virtue. For years, the rebels had championed the raw power of vice as the spark that ignited innovation, while the establishment clung to a sanitised version of virtue as the only path to order. Now, however, a peculiar alchemy was beginning to take shape—a convergence where the edges of vice and virtue softened, intertwined, and coalesced into something altogether new.

It began subtly, almost imperceptibly, like a shift in the air that foretold an approaching storm. In the back alleys of Luminex, where neon lights flickered against crumbling brick, the rebellious graffiti that once screamed of unbridled chaos now carried hints of a measured grace. Phrases like "Embrace the Shadow, Honour the Light" and "Flaws are the Seeds of Wisdom" began to appear alongside the anarchic slogans of old. These new declarations hinted at an emerging truth: that the virtues championed by the establishment and the vices celebrated by the dissenters were not entirely oppositional, but two halves of the same tumultuous coin.

At a nondescript café on the fringe of the corporate district, a small gathering of thinkers, artists, and renegades met over strong coffee and even stronger opinions. Among them was Helena, a former ethics professor whose career had been upended by her controversial views on morality, and now, in the midst of revolution, she had become a reluctant bridge between the two worlds. "For too long," she said, her voice calm yet resonant, "we have painted virtue and vice as absolute opposites. But what if our most authentic selves are born from the tension between them? What if our capacity to rebel is enhanced by the very values we once sought to uphold?" Her words, delivered with an ironic smile and a glimmer of hope, sent ripples of quiet agreement through the room.

Across town, in an art studio cluttered with discarded canvases and bursts of splattered color, Jessa—whose murals had become symbols of pure defiance—was experimenting with a new style. No longer content with the overt expressions of chaos, she began to infuse her work with elements of classical beauty and structured design. In one large piece, a tumultuous storm of vivid hues merged seamlessly into the delicate curves of an ancient Greek column. The juxtaposition was jarring yet mesmerizing—a visual manifestation of the paradox that had taken root in the city: that vice and virtue might, in fact, share common ground. "Perhaps," she mused aloud to a small group of onlookers, "our rebellion doesn't require the complete rejection of all order. Instead, it might be about reclaiming the order that exists within chaos, and the chaos that exists within order."

This notion of convergence began to echo through the underground channels. Digital forums once dedicated solely to the glorification of wild, unrestrained vice now hosted debates on the merits of balance, on the possibility that virtue—if redefined in honest, unpretentious terms—could coexist with, or even enhance, the creative energy of vice. The discussions were heated, filled with dark sarcasm and bitter laughter, yet underneath the surface was a budding curiosity. People who had always seen themselves as either radical or righteous were beginning to wonder if the boundaries were not as fixed as they had assumed.

In a crowded subway car one rainy evening, Theo found himself in an impromptu conversation with a suited businessman whose eyes betrayed a weariness born of endless conformity. The man, whose carefully curated image had once been his shield against the world, admitted, "I've always believed that virtue was what made society work. But lately, I see that our rigid definitions of good have left little room for real life—messy, unpredictable life." Theo, ever the reflective poet, nodded slowly. "Perhaps our virtues are like scaffolding," he offered, his tone soft yet penetrating, "supporting us until we learn to build without them. In our flaws, in our unbridled impulses, there's a kind of truth that no sanitised rule can capture." The businessman's brow furrowed as he considered this, a spark of reluctant understanding kindling behind his eyes.

As the days wore on, the city became a living laboratory for this emerging synthesis. The daily routines of Luminex were punctuated not only by acts of overt rebellion, but by subtle, almost imperceptible shifts. In neighborhoods that had once echoed with the hollow clatter of conformity, people began to display small signs of their newfound duality. A tailor, whose hands had long stitched uniform suits for faceless corporates, started experimenting with vibrant, unconventional patterns that merged classic cuts with daring asymmetry. A group of office workers, tired of the mindless repetition of their daily grind, began to organize secret lunchtime "mindfulness sessions" where they discussed not only productivity hacks but also the importance of embracing imperfection in their work—and in themselves.

At The Crucible, the epicenter of the rebellion, the atmosphere grew charged with an almost surreal blend of jubilance and introspection. In one corner of the repurposed warehouse, a large projector screened a montage of moments from the recent Day of Divergence—a vivid tapestry of flash mobs, defiant murals, and spontaneous speeches that had rocked the city. The images, raw and unfiltered, were accompanied by a slow, haunting melody that seemed to capture the bittersweet irony of a revolution that was as much about reclaiming humanity as it was about tearing down oppressive structures. "We are at a crossroads," Helena declared to the gathered crowd, her voice echoing through the cavernous space. "For years, we have celebrated vice as the engine of innovation, while virtue was relegated to a sterile ideal. Now, we stand on the brink of understanding that our strength lies not in choosing one over the other, but in embracing the paradox that both reside within us. It is in the convergence of these forces that we find our true power."

Her words resonated with every rebel in the room. They began to see that the struggle was not simply about destruction—it was about transformation. The rebellion was evolving from an all-out assault on the old order to a more nuanced, reflective movement that sought to integrate the best of both worlds. The dark, unbridled energy of vice was tempered by the warmth of genuine, albeit humble, virtue; the chaos of rebellion found its counterbalance in moments of quiet empathy and understanding.

In the following days, as this new philosophy spread through the digital underground and into the streets of Luminex, the movement began to witness tangible changes. Digital platforms that had once been the exclusive playgrounds of anarchic thought now featured creative collaborations between radical artists and pragmatic thinkers. A viral video emerged of a group of rebels collaborating with a retired schoolteacher to create a public art installation that combined traditional calligraphy with wild, explosive street art—a symbolic merging of the old and the new, the virtuous and the vice-ridden.

The installation, which took place in a central park, featured a massive mural depicting a phoenix rising from a bed of broken chains. Its wings were painted with the soft, intricate patterns of classical art, yet its body was rendered in bold, chaotic strokes that spoke of raw, untamed emotion. Passersby stopped to stare, many moved by the unexpected beauty of this synthesis—a visual reminder that from the ashes of conformity, a new order could indeed emerge.

Amid these converging trends, individual stories of transformation began to surface. Marcus, once known for his bitter diatribes against a society of drones, found himself softening his rhetoric as he encountered moments of genuine compassion among his fellow rebels. He recalled a chance encounter with an elderly woman in a narrow alley, whose simple act of sharing a warm smile had momentarily bridged the gap between the harsh world of survival and the tender possibility of care. “Perhaps,” he later confessed in one of his digital posts, “our greatest rebellion is not merely to defy, but to embrace—to allow the light of virtue to shine even in the darkest corners of our existence.” His reflection was met with an outpouring of support, as many in the digital community began to share their own stories of finding unexpected kindness amidst chaos.

As the movement matured, it became clear that the convergence of vice and virtue was not a momentary aberration, but the natural evolution of a society that had long been polarized by extremes. The rebels came to understand that while unbridled vice had indeed sparked the initial flames of rebellion, it was the integration of humble, authentic virtue that would sustain the revolution in the long run. In embracing their flaws and acknowledging that even within the chaos lay the potential for order, they forged a new path—a path defined not by rigid binaries, but by a spectrum of possibilities that celebrated the full range of human experience.

In quiet corners of Luminex, in digital forums filled with unedited truths, the dialogue deepened. People who had once dismissed the movement as nothing more than anarchic ranting began to see the beauty in a balanced approach. They recognized that while the state’s sanitised vision of virtue had often suffocated creativity, there was room for an authentic, lived morality—one that honoured compassion, empathy, and resilience without demanding perfection. The idea that vice and virtue could coexist, interweaving to form a more robust, humane tapestry, gradually took root in the hearts of many.

And so, as the days turned into weeks, the city began to transform not just in its public spaces but in the very consciousness of its inhabitants. The convergence of vice and virtue emerged as a rallying cry—a call to embrace all facets of one’s nature, to recognize that our imperfections, when integrated with our noblest aspirations, could create a foundation for a society that was both dynamic and humane.

In that evolving dialogue, Helena's earlier words continued to resonate. "True power," she had once said, "is found in the balance between defiance and compassion, between the unyielding spirit of rebellion and the quiet strength of genuine virtue." The rebels began to see that their fight was not solely against the oppressive forces of conformity, but also a quest to rediscover a more authentic, nuanced understanding of what it meant to be human.

As the convergence took hold, even the state's relentless efforts to clamp down on dissent inadvertently fed into the movement's narrative. Every public crackdown, every sterile press release, was reinterpreted by the digital underground as evidence of the old order's fragility—a sign that beneath the veneer of order, the human spirit was too wild to be contained. The more the establishment struggled to enforce its narrow vision of virtue, the more the people embraced the full spectrum of their nature, blending the sharp edges of vice with the soft, redeeming glow of compassion.

In this way, Luminex found itself at the crossroads of transformation—a city where the once-clear lines between right and wrong, good and bad, had blurred into a vibrant mosaic of lived experience. The convergence of vice and virtue was not a surrender to chaos, but a deliberate act of creation—a rebellion that recognized that only by accepting the entirety of our humanity could we hope to forge a future that was as authentic as it was revolutionary.

The revolution was no longer simply a collision of extremes; it had begun to smooth its edges, revealing a complex tapestry where the stark boundaries between vice and virtue blurred into a spectrum of possibility. In the weeks following the initial stirrings of convergence, the citizens of Luminex found themselves inexplicably drawn to experiences that defied simple categorization. What had once been defined as pure vice—a wild, untamed disregard for the rules—now revealed hidden layers of genuine virtue when practiced with purpose and awareness.

Likewise, the virtues once held up as moral beacons, rigid and pristine, started to show their own vulnerabilities and contradictions when stripped of their hypocrisy.

In a refurbished art gallery located in a former industrial complex, an exhibit titled "Duality Unchained" opened to a modest but curious crowd. The gallery walls were awash in an eclectic mix of works—stark photographs, sprawling murals, and intricate sculptures—that illustrated the interplay between chaos and order. One striking installation, for instance, featured a shattered mirror arranged in a circular pattern on the floor. Each fragment bore a handwritten message: "Every crack tells a story," "Imperfection is truth," "From ruin, we are reborn." Visitors wandered slowly, pausing as the interplay of light and shadow transformed these fragments into a mosaic that seemed to capture the entire spectrum of human experience.

Helena, once a professor of ethics and now a reluctant mediator between the old and the new, wandered among the exhibits. Her eyes, thoughtful and tempered by years of academic rigor, now sparkled with a curiosity that defied her former certainties. Standing before a painting that depicted a tumultuous storm merging into a serene landscape, she murmured to herself, "In the heart of chaos lies a strange form of order—one that's messy, unpredictable, yet undeniably real." Her voice, carrying both irony and an unexpected tenderness, drew the attention of a young artist nearby who introduced himself as Theo. "I always thought that virtue was about perfection," Theo admitted, his tone wistful yet defiant. "But now, I see that it's about resilience—the ability to rise, even when we're broken." Their conversation, rich with philosophical musing and dark humor, encapsulated the essence of this new convergence.

Elsewhere, on a bustling street corner in a neighborhood once synonymous with oppressive sameness, a pop-up performance took center stage. A group of performers, their costumes a riotous blend of vintage elegance and streetwise grit, staged a dramatic reenactment of a fabled confrontation between the embodiments of Vice and Virtue. The "Vice" character, clad in a leather jacket adorned with rebellious patches and exuding a roguish charm, clashed with "Virtue," who appeared in crisp, almost ostentatious attire—a symbol of the sanitised ideal. But as the skit unfolded, the scripted antagonism gave way to a surprising, almost tender dialogue. Vice, with a sardonic grin, declared, "I've always been seen as the scoundrel, the reckless force. Yet without me, your precious order would be nothing but a hollow, static dream." Virtue, her voice softening, retorted, "And I, labeled the beacon of morality, have long concealed the cost of that so-called order—a price paid in lost passion, in the sacrifice of spontaneity." The performance, filled with biting satire and subtle irony, left the audience both laughing and introspective—a poignant reminder that the dichotomy they had once clung to was rapidly dissolving.

Digital spaces continued to serve as the lifeblood of this new movement. The underground platform championed by Silas and Marisol had evolved into a vibrant forum where dissent was celebrated as art and every post became a piece of the evolving narrative. In a thread titled "Our Flawed Light," users shared stories of personal transformation—tales of people who had once feared to deviate from the norm but had found a strange, invigorating freedom in embracing their own contradictions. One post recounted how a middle-aged businessman, long ensnared by the pressures of corporate conformity, had quit his job to pursue painting. His photos of raw, emotionally charged canvases resonated with thousands. Another story told of a schoolteacher who, tired of preaching rote lessons, had started an after-hours poetry club that explored the messy realities of life. These digital confessions, raw and unpolished, merged into a collective chorus that celebrated the messy synthesis of vice and virtue.

The cityscape itself, too, began to mirror this internal transformation. In neighborhoods that had long been uniform and unyielding, vibrant street art emerged that reflected the newfound complexity of human identity. One striking mural on the side of an aging building depicted a single, imposing tree whose roots and branches intertwined with symbols of both rebellion and tradition—a spiral of flames and ancient glyphs that symbolized the eternal interplay of chaos and order. The mural's caption read simply: "Out of our imperfections, we are whole." It was a visual manifesto that resonated with passersby, challenging them to see beauty not in pristine order, but in the untamed splendor of life's contradictions.

At The Crucible—a former warehouse turned cultural epicenter—the atmosphere was electric with anticipation. The rebels gathered for yet another round of discussions, this time focusing on how to institutionalize the lessons learned from their journey thus far. Lena, who had emerged as one of the most passionate leaders of The Unbound, addressed the assembly with a measured yet fervent tone. "We've spent years railing against a system that forces us into neat categories," she began, her gaze sweeping over the sea of faces lit by the glow of flickering bulbs. "But what if our strength lies not in outright rejection, but in the integration of everything we are—both the wild, untamed parts that society calls vice and the disciplined, empathetic parts that we once misinterpreted as virtue? True liberation will come when we embrace our full humanity, without shame or pretense." Her words, laden with both hope and dark realism, stirred a murmur of agreement. They realized that by reconciling these opposing forces within themselves, they could create a more robust foundation for the revolution—a synthesis that could withstand the onslaught of a system desperate to maintain its outdated order.

In the days that followed, collaborative projects sprouted like wildflowers in unexpected places. Artists teamed up with philosophers; technologists joined forces with community organizers; even some former enforcers of conformity—disillusioned bureaucrats who had once been part of the state machinery—lent their expertise to the cause. One project, dubbed "The Harmony Initiative," aimed to create interactive installations in public spaces that would invite citizens to share their own stories of contradiction. At a busy public square, a large interactive screen allowed passersby to record short messages about their personal struggles and triumphs—how they balanced the demands of societal expectations with their own intrinsic desires. The collected messages, displayed in a constantly shifting mosaic, became a living testament to the complexity of modern identity—a reminder that every individual was an amalgamation of defiant vice and nurtured virtue.

Amid these endeavors, Helena continued to serve as a thoughtful mediator between disparate factions. In a series of public lectures held in the once-dreary halls of a local community center, she explored the historical evolution of moral philosophy, drawing parallels between ancient debates on human nature and the current crisis in Luminex. "Our ancestors wrestled with the duality of man long before our modern systems reduced us to mere numbers on a spreadsheet," she explained in one lecture, her voice measured and sincere. "What we are witnessing now is not the collapse of society, but its transformation—a reawakening to the idea that our imperfections are not flaws to be eradicated but virtues to be embraced." Her lectures, broadcast via the digital network, drew a surprising number of viewers—both young and old—who found solace in her balanced perspective.

The convergence of vice and virtue soon spilled over into everyday interactions. In the corridors of once-sterile office buildings, employees began to share their stories of personal rebellion in hushed, conspiratorial tones. A middle manager, who had long been the embodiment of corporate efficiency, confided in a colleague that he had started writing a blog about the absurdity of office life—mixing sarcastic commentary with poignant insights about the human need for imperfection. His posts, which were circulated discreetly among the staff, slowly chipped away at the rigid narratives that had long defined their existence. Even the city's youth, once dismissed as mere rebels, began to engage in thoughtful dialogues about the nature of morality, questioning whether the old labels of "good" and "bad" were not as clear-cut as they had been taught.

Digital art collectives sprang up in the online spaces, where creators shared works that blended chaotic imagery with classical motifs. One viral piece featured a classical statue whose chiseled features were overlaid with spray-painted symbols of modern rebellion—a deliberate fusion of the timeless and the transient. Comments flooded in, with viewers debating the meaning of the work, some praising its raw honesty and others mocking its apparent contradiction. Yet, even in the midst of such polarized reactions, there was a growing awareness that the convergence was more than a fleeting trend—it was a fundamental shift in the way people perceived themselves and the world around them.

By the time evening fell on a particularly charged day in Luminex, the city itself seemed to be humming with the energy of a new possibility. In a public park transformed into an open-air forum, a spontaneous debate unfolded. Participants from all walks of life—students, elderly residents, former government officials—engaged in a lively discussion about the future of morality. The debate was punctuated by sharp wit, dark humor, and moments of unexpected tenderness. One elderly gentleman, his voice trembling with a mix of nostalgia and defiance, declared, "I used to think that virtue was the preservation of our legacy. But now I see that our true legacy is the raw, unedited truth of our existence—the courage to embrace our entire selves, imperfections and all." His words, simple yet profound, resonated with the gathered crowd, igniting a wave of applause that mingled with tears and laughter.

As night descended once more, the digital sphere continued to buzz with the convergence of ideas. Memes, videos, and forum posts celebrated the union of vice and virtue, each piece a digital artifact of this unprecedented synthesis. The digital platform, now a thriving ecosystem of unfiltered creativity, reflected the complexity of human nature in every scroll and click. Users shared their newfound perspectives, acknowledging that the journey toward authenticity was not about choosing between the extremes but about forging a new path that honoured both.

In the midst of this turbulent yet hopeful landscape, the rebels of Luminex felt a cautious optimism. They realized that while the road ahead was still fraught with challenges, the blending of vice and virtue had opened a door to a richer, more inclusive understanding of what it meant to be human. In embracing the messy, unpredictable aspects of their nature, they were not abandoning morality—instead, they were reimagining it, transforming it into a living, breathing force that could empower rather than restrict.

As the convergence deepened, every individual in Luminex began to understand that true progress was found not in rigid adherence to outdated norms, but in the courage to live authentically—by accepting the darkness alongside the light. And as the digital voices merged with the vibrant pulse of the streets, a new narrative emerged—a narrative that celebrated the full spectrum of human experience, where vice met virtue in a delicate, dynamic dance of transformation.

As the digital echoes of rebellion spread further through Luminex, the city's inhabitants—once entrenched in rigid moral binaries—found themselves facing a profound, internal reckoning. What had begun as isolated acts of defiance in alleyways and underground forums was now catalyzing personal transformations that rippled outward into every aspect of daily life. People who had once clung to the black-and-white narratives of right and wrong now discovered that the truth lay in a complex tapestry of contradictions.

In a modest neighborhood café that had seen better days, where the faded upholstery bore the marks of years of routine and resignation, a small group of regulars gathered around a stained wooden table. Among them was Daniel, a middle-aged schoolteacher known for his once-proud adherence to a strict moral code. Over the months of underground discussions and clandestine readings of The Unbound's manifesto, Daniel's rigid views had begun to crumble like old plaster. His hands, weathered by years of chalk dust and lesson plans, trembled slightly as he recounted a personal epiphany.

"I spent my life teaching that there was a clear line between good and evil," Daniel confessed, his voice a mix of nostalgia and bitter humor. "But now I realize that even in the acts I once condemned, there was a spark—a raw, unfiltered truth that made me question everything I'd ever believed. I used to think that vice was a dangerous aberration. Now, I see that it holds pieces of our humanity that we've been forced to hide." His eyes glistened with unshed tears as he added, "It's as if the more we try to polish our souls, the more we lose the very imperfections that make us real."

Across the table, a young woman named Mira—whose vibrant tattoos and unapologetic attitude had made her a symbol of defiant self-expression—nodded in agreement. Mira had long lived at the intersection of rebellion and vulnerability. Once, her life had been a continuous act of defiance, marked by wild nights and reckless choices. But over time, she discovered that there was beauty in balance. "I used to live like every day was a dare," Mira said, her tone both sardonic and soft. "But the dare isn't just to shock the world; it's to discover what part of me is worth preserving, even when I let go of all the constraints. I've found that the very things we call vices—our passions, our impulsiveness—when tempered with empathy and understanding, can evolve into a kind of virtue. It's messy, but it's genuine."

Their conversation flowed easily, as if the weight of their shared experiences dissolved the boundaries between their individual stories. Outside, the city was busy with its own quiet metamorphosis. The ultra-modern glass towers of downtown now glinted with unexpected graffiti—each tag, each carefully scrawled phrase was no longer a mere act of defiance, but a testament to an emerging philosophy. On one particularly striking wall near the financial district, the words "Beauty Lies in the Broken" were emblazoned in bold, erratic strokes. The message resonated with passersby, who paused in their hurried commutes to take in this raw reinterpretation of aesthetic truth.

Not far from that wall, in the dim light of an art studio converted from an old factory, Jessa continued her creative experiments. She was reworking one of her earlier murals—once a stark celebration of anarchic vice—by integrating classical elements and subtle hues that evoked both chaos and calm. The piece depicted a tumultuous sea gradually giving way to a serene horizon, its waves interlaced with symbols of both rebellion and tradition. As she painted, Jessa murmured to herself, "Maybe this is what convergence feels like—the wild surge of emotion tempered by the delicate brush of history. Our world isn't either-or; it's a layered canvas of conflicting truths." Her eyes, reflecting the interplay of light and shadow on the mural, shone with a newfound tenderness as she embraced the idea that authenticity could exist even in the spaces between extremes.

Meanwhile, on the digital front, the underground platform continued to serve as a vital hub for those exploring this emerging synthesis. Threads that had once been dedicated solely to outraged proclamations of freedom now carried thoughtful exchanges on how personal experiences of vice could merge with moments of profound moral insight. One viral post recounted the journey of a former corporate lawyer who, after years of strict conformity, had left his lucrative career to pursue art. His raw narrative—filled with regret for the lost years and joy for the new, unfiltered life he had embraced—became a rallying cry for those grappling with the duality of their own identities. Comments flooded in, some praising his honesty, others debating the nuances of a morality that was as multifaceted as the human condition. In a space once characterized by black-and-white slogans, shades of gray began to dominate—a testament to the growing consensus that authenticity was found in the interplay of contradictions.

In a public lecture organized by The Unbound at a reclaimed community center, Helena returned to the stage. Her lecture, titled "The Intertwined Paths of Vice and Virtue," was a masterful blend of historical insights and contemporary reflections. Dressed in a simple outfit that belied the intellectual weight of her words, she addressed an audience that ranged from disillusioned youths to aged intellectuals. "We have long been taught that vice is the enemy, a force to be eradicated," Helena began, her voice steady and resonant. “Yet history teaches us that some of the greatest innovations have sprung not from strict adherence to moral codes, but from the creative spark that emerges in moments of moral ambiguity. It is in the space where our darkest impulses meet our highest ideals that true evolution occurs.” Her lecture, laced with dry humor and incisive critique, left the audience both challenged and inspired. For many, it was the first time they felt validated in their internal conflicts—a recognition that the duality within was not a flaw, but a wellspring of potential.

As the days turned into weeks, the convergence of vice and virtue began to manifest in unexpected ways throughout Luminex. In one upscale neighborhood known for its ostentatious displays of wealth and rigid adherence to etiquette, a series of spontaneous gatherings started to occur in public parks. These were not the raucous protests of earlier days, but more intimate, reflective assemblies where people shared stories of personal transformation. A retired banker recounted how he had once prided himself on his disciplined life, only to later realize that his obsession with order had rendered him incapable of experiencing joy. “It was only when I allowed myself to be vulnerable—that is, to embrace a little chaos—that I truly started to live,” he admitted, his voice soft with both regret and relief. His confession, shared in a circle of attentive neighbors, marked a quiet revolution in a place once dominated by silent conformity.

Elsewhere, in a busy metropolitan square, a live art performance unfolded. A group of mixed-media artists, in collaboration with classical musicians, staged an elaborate piece titled “Symphony of the Sundered.” The performance combined traditional instruments with impromptu soundscapes created by everyday objects—metallic clangs, rhythmic drips of rainwater, the distant hum of city life. The resulting melody was both jarring and beautiful, a sonic representation of a society in transition. In the midst of the performance, a charismatic poet took center stage and recited verses that spoke of redemption found in the act of self-acceptance. “We are not defined by the rigid lines drawn by others," he intoned, his voice carrying over the crowd, "but by the beautiful mess of our own making. In our imperfections, we find the courage to be free." The audience, a diverse tapestry of skeptics and believers, responded with a mixture of applause and introspective silence—a moment of collective understanding that the old dichotomies were dissolving before their eyes.

Digital conversations continued to be a crucible for new ideas. Threads on the underground platform grew longer and more nuanced, with users sharing personal essays, poems, and even short films that explored the theme of convergence. One particularly poignant video featured a montage of individuals from different walks of life—corporate executives, street performers, teachers, and students—sharing brief statements about the contradictions they had learned to embrace. The montage ended with a striking message: "Our strength lies in our complexity." It was a simple sentiment, but one that resonated deeply with those who had long felt the sting of being forced into a single narrative.

Amid these cultural shifts, the state's response continued to intensify. Law enforcement agencies, still reeling from the unexpected tide of dissent, ramped up their efforts to restore the old order. Yet, every crackdown seemed only to underline the growing discontent. Video footage of peaceful protests and quiet acts of resistance circulated widely, fueling debates about the true nature of freedom and control. In one instance, a public relations officer for the government was forced to address the outcry over a particularly heavy-handed raid on a neighborhood art festival. His scripted apologies and sanitised explanations were met with scathing rebuttals online, where citizens marveled at the state's inability to understand that true order could not be imposed from above—it had to emerge organically from within.

Back at The Crucible, as Helena's lecture concluded and the community center's lights dimmed for the night, the rebels gathered for an informal debrief. The mood was one of cautious optimism tempered by the sobering reality of the challenges ahead. Lena, ever the resilient leader, summed up the day's events with a wry smile. "We're witnessing something remarkable," she said, her voice low and steady. "For the first time in a long while, it feels like the lines between what we once believed were polar opposites are blurring. Vice and virtue—they're not the enemy of each other, but different notes in the same symphony. And if we can learn to play that symphony in harmony, then maybe, just maybe, we can build a future that honours all facets of who we are."

Her words were met with quiet applause—a mix of exhaustion, hope, and the fierce determination of those who had tasted both the bitterness of repression and the sweetness of liberation. As the night deepened and the rebels slowly dispersed into the labyrinth of the city, each carried with them a piece of this newfound convergence—a belief that the future was not a choice between extremes, but a journey through the rich spectrum of human experience.

In the early hours before dawn, as Luminex slumbered under the faint glow of streetlights and the soft hum of distant traffic, individual acts of convergence continued to unfold. A lone musician, whose heart had been broken by the monotony of corporate life, played a mournful tune on an old saxophone in a deserted alley. His notes, winding and bittersweet, resonated with the realization that beauty could be found even in the midst of despair. Across town, a former executive—once a staunch defender of the rigid moral order—quietly donated his savings to support community art projects that celebrated raw, unedited creativity. In his own small way, he was beginning to understand that his past adherence to a sanitised version of virtue had only hollowed him out, and that real fulfillment lay in embracing the full complexity of his being.

As dawn approached, the digital realm buzzed with renewed activity. Posts celebrating the convergence of vice and virtue became a trending topic on the underground platform, with hashtags like #WholeAndBroken and #ComplexFreedom spreading rapidly. People shared their journeys—tales of personal transformation that detailed how letting go of rigid self-expectations had opened doors to deeper connections and more genuine creativity. In these stories, the rebels found validation for their own struggles—a reminder that the fight was not merely external, but deeply personal. Each shared confession was a spark that illuminated the path toward a more inclusive, authentic society.

In one particularly moving post, a young woman described how her years of self-repression had given way to a blossoming of creativity when she finally allowed herself to embrace her so-called vices. "I used to believe that to be virtuous was to be flawless," she wrote, "but I've learned that every misstep, every moment of unbridled passion, is a thread in the rich tapestry of who I am. Now, I celebrate my contradictions as much as my strengths." Her words, raw and unfiltered, resonated with thousands, each comment a small declaration that perfection was not the goal, but the journey itself.

By the time the sun finally peeked over the horizon, Luminex had transformed into a living testament to the convergence of its disparate souls. The city's landscape, once dominated by the stark contrast of vice and virtue, now bore the subtle, intertwined signatures of both—a mural here, a viral video there, a shared moment of quiet defiance that spoke volumes. The convergence was not a neatly packaged solution, but a messy, ongoing process—a dynamic interplay of rebellion and redemption that each individual carried within them.

As dusk turned to a deep indigo, the city of Luminex seemed to exhale a long-held breath—a sigh that carried both the weight of its past divisions and the hopeful promise of transformation. The convergence of vice and virtue had not been a sudden epiphany but a gradual evolution, a painstaking reconciliation of two forces once seen as irreconcilable. Now, in the waning hours before a new dawn, this synthesis was on full display, not as a neatly packaged ideal but as a raw, living tapestry woven from every contradiction, every scar, and every moment of fierce rebellion.

In the sprawling public square that had once served as the emblem of corporate order, a massive mural now stretched along an entire building facade. The artwork was a breathtaking collision of styles and eras: classical motifs intertwined with explosive street art, intricate calligraphy merging with chaotic splashes of neon. At the center of the mural, a phoenix—its wings an elegant blend of organic curves and jagged, spray-painted edges—rose from a bed of shattered chains. Below it, in a swirling collage of vibrant letters, was inscribed the phrase, "Our Imperfections Are Our Strength." For passersby, the mural was both a defiant challenge to the old order and a visual hymn to the beauty of human complexity. Every brushstroke, every layer of paint seemed to pulse with the collective heartbeat of a city that had finally learned to embrace its own contradictions.

Across the square, a makeshift stage had been set up for what was billed as the final act of the convergence celebration. Here, in front of a throng of citizens whose eyes glimmered with anticipation and defiance, Helena returned to the microphone. Once a respected professor of ethics and now a revered voice of this new movement, she stood poised and resolute amid the ambient hum of the crowd. "We have long been taught to fear the messy, unpredictable parts of ourselves," she began, her voice calm yet imbued with passionate urgency. "For years, vice was demonized as the enemy of order, and virtue exalted as the only path to salvation. But tonight, we reject that false dichotomy. Our true power lies in embracing every facet of our humanity—both the darkness and the light, the chaos and the compassion. In our convergence, we find a strength that is as raw and unfiltered as life itself."

Her words, resonating through the cool evening air, were met with a moment of profound silence before the crowd erupted into rapturous applause. In that instant, it was clear: the convergence was not simply a philosophical debate—it was a lived, breathing reality that had already reshaped the soul of Luminex.

From the digital realm, the underground platform's latest posts flashed across public screens in nearby cafés and subway stations. Images of personal transformations, of individuals who had once been trapped in the sterile confines of conformity now celebrating their inner complexities, were shared widely. One post featured a former corporate lawyer turned street muralist, whose work depicted not only the raw power of vice but also tender, evocative scenes of forgiveness and connection. Another showed a group of elderly citizens—long resigned to the drudgery of routine—dancing in a public park under strings of colorful lights, their faces radiant with joy and rebellion. These digital narratives, unedited and fiercely honest, had become the pulse of the city—a testament to the power of unfiltered truth.

In a cozy, dimly lit room at The Crucible—the revered cultural epicenter that had nurtured the rebellion—the leaders of The Unbound gathered for a final planning session. The room, alive with the soft buzz of digital devices and the murmurs of determined conversation, was a crucible of ideas and emotions. Lena, whose journey from a corporate drone to a fearless revolutionary had inspired countless acts of defiance, addressed the assembly one last time before the new day would fully break. "Our struggle was never about choosing one extreme over the other," she said, her eyes scanning the room with a blend of empathy and steely resolve. "It was about finding the truth in the tension between opposites. Today, we celebrate the union of vice and virtue, and we commit to carrying this spirit forward into every corner of our lives. Let our imperfections be the brushstrokes that paint a future unbound by old rules."

Her words were punctuated by nods and murmurs of agreement—a collective affirmation that the revolution was evolving from isolated acts of rebellion into a comprehensive reimagining of society. In that room, ideas flowed freely: plans for public art installations that would continue to challenge conventional beauty, proposals for digital forums that would amplify every unsanitised voice, and discussions on how to integrate the lessons learned from personal transformation into the broader fabric of the city.

Outside, as the final hours of night waned and the first hints of dawn touched the horizon, the energy of the convergence was palpable. Across Luminex, small, deliberate acts of individuality had become the norm. In a neighborhood that had once been draped in uniform shades of gray, residents began to display subtle signs of their reclaimed self-expression—a hand-painted sign on a door proclaiming "I Am More Than My Labels," a young woman sporting a boldly mismatched outfit, a street artist's mural that boldly declared "Embrace Your Flaws." These were not isolated moments; they were the living proof that the old, oppressive structures were giving way to a more vibrant, inclusive reality.

In one particularly moving scene, an elderly man who had spent decades as a stern enforcer of conventional wisdom was seen in a public square, quietly reading a handwritten note that he had found pinned to a community bulletin board. The note, penned in a shaky yet sincere hand, read: "In every crack of conformity, there is a window to freedom." The man's eyes softened as he clutched the note, and for a brief moment, it was as if his entire life of rigid adherence had been upended by the simple, powerful truth of the message. It was a small act of rebellion that spoke volumes—an acknowledgment that even the staunchest proponents of order could find beauty in the chaotic, unedited facets of life.

Elsewhere, at a makeshift stage in a renovated park, a poet with a voice both rough and tender took the mic. "We are not bound by the narrow confines of what society deems acceptable," he declared, his words resonating like a solemn vow. "Our virtues are not defined by perfection, and our vices are not condemned by default. Instead, we are whole in our contradictions—every flaw, every misstep, every unbridled moment of passion is a testament to our humanity. In our convergence, we find the strength to rebuild, to reinvent, and to reimagine a world where every part of us is celebrated." The crowd, a sea of faces lit by the soft glow of streetlights and the fervour of shared purpose, listened intently, their applause a gentle but powerful tribute to the transformative message.

As the night slowly yielded to the early light of dawn, Helena emerged onto a quiet balcony overlooking the city. The view was a collage of dark silhouettes against a gradually brightening sky—a reminder of the endless struggle and the fragile hope that defined their revolution. In that serene, reflective moment, she allowed herself a wry smile. "We have learned that the truth isn't found in the extremes," she murmured softly, almost to herself, "but in the spaces between—the cracks where the light seeps in and makes the darkness bearable." It was a moment of intimate revelation that encapsulated the journey of convergence: a recognition that real change was not a matter of choosing sides, but of embracing the full, messy spectrum of life.

By the time the sun's rays began to break over the horizon, the city of Luminex was already transformed—not in a single sweeping revolution, but in a mosaic of small, deliberate acts that together forged a new identity. The convergence of vice and virtue had not erased the past or nullified the struggles that had led to this moment. Instead, it had woven them into a rich, complex narrative where every tear and every scar was honoured as part of the human story.

In that final, glorious morning, as the rebels dispersed into the awakening city, every face reflected a quiet certainty: that the future was not a choice between extremes, but a celebration of the complete, unvarnished self. The chains of old conformity had been battered and broken by the relentless, uncompromising power of authenticity. And though the journey ahead would undoubtedly hold further challenges, the spirit of convergence—the delicate, dynamic dance between vice and virtue—would guide them forward into a world where every soul was free to shine in its unfiltered, brilliant imperfection.

CHAPTER EIGHT

The Price of Progress : Consequences and Rewards

Luminex was no longer the pristine, controlled city it once appeared to be. Its sleek towers and manicured streets had been upended by the tumult of rebellion—by the raw, unfiltered surge of change that had swept through its heart. But as the rebels' bold ideas began to reshape society, a deeper truth emerged: progress, for all its promise, demanded a heavy toll. Every act of defiance, every shattered chain of conformity, bore its own consequences—some painful, others transformative, and many irrevocably intertwined.

In the early days following the uprising, the streets of Luminex buzzed with triumphant cries and ecstatic celebration. Murals bloomed on once-sterile walls, graffiti became the language of dissent, and every public space transformed into a canvas for expression. For a time, it seemed that the cost of revolution was being paid in brilliant bursts of color and unbridled joy. But as days turned into weeks, the darker side of progress began to assert itself.

For many of the rebels, the price was personal. Lena, who had risen from the shackles of a soulless corporate existence to become one of the movement's most impassioned leaders, found that each act of rebellion chipped away not only at the oppressive structures of Luminex but also at the familiar comforts of her former life. The endless nights spent planning underground meetings, the constant threat of state reprisal, and the painful alienation from friends and family—all had left her marked. In quiet moments before dawn, when the adrenaline faded and the weight of solitude pressed in, Lena would catch her reflection in a rain-soaked window and see not the fierce rebel leader that the world now knew, but a woman burdened by sacrifice. "Freedom," she once murmured in the silence of her apartment, "is a double-edged sword. Every victory in the streets comes at the cost of something deeply personal." Her words, heavy with the gravity of loss, echoed the reality that progress was never free—it demanded that one give up parts of oneself to ignite change.

Yet, it wasn't only personal relationships that suffered. Across Luminex, the cultural landscape was in flux, and the consequences of revolution rippled outwards into every corner of society. In neighborhoods that had once epitomized the comfort of routine, residents found themselves disoriented by the sudden influx of unfiltered expression. Elderly citizens, who had relied on the stability of long-held traditions, wandered confused amid walls adorned with defiant slogans and vivid murals that challenged everything they had been taught to value. For them, the relentless barrage of change was both invigorating and deeply unsettling—a stark reminder that the familiar had been irrevocably altered.

Even the digital world, once a sanctuary of unedited, anarchic truth, began to show signs of wear. The underground platform that had become the rallying cry of the rebellion was now awash with a constant stream of raw confessions, images of rebellion, and impassioned debates. But the ceaseless flow of unfiltered content, while exhilarating at first, started to take its toll. Users reported feelings of fatigue, disillusionment, and even a creeping sense of isolation. It seemed that in the pursuit of authenticity, some had forgotten that the truth, when laid bare too relentlessly, could be as painful as it was liberating. "We've been burning with passion," one user lamented in a late-night post, "but now the flames have left scars that run deeper than any system of control ever could." The comment struck a chord, resonating with those who had felt that the raw energy of rebellion was beginning to transform into a relentless, exhausting burden.

Amid these personal and communal consequences, there were also unforeseen rewards—moments of transformation that testified to the inherent power of risk and defiance. In the heart of a battered, graffiti-splattered neighborhood, a small community art project emerged from the rubble of despair. Local artisans, previously resigned to the gray monotony of survival, began to collaborate on vibrant public installations. One such project, dubbed "The Ledger of Change," invited residents to record their personal stories of loss, failure, and unexpected triumph. Over time, the once-sterile walls of a derelict building became a living museum of raw human experience—a testament to the fact that every scar and every setback held the potential to become a badge of honour. "Every crack in the façade tells a story," the inscription read in bold, hand-painted letters. "Every wound is a doorway to growth." This evolving mural, a collective diary of the city's metamorphosis, reminded its viewers that while progress demanded sacrifice, it also cultivated a deeper, more resilient form of beauty.

At a dimly lit café in one of the city's more turbulent districts, a group of rebels gathered to share their experiences over bitter coffee and whispered conversations. Marcus, known for his acerbic wit and unyielding commitment to defiance, recounted a particularly harrowing encounter with the state's enforcers. "They came like vultures, expecting us to cower in fear," he said, his voice a low, measured growl. "Instead, we stood our ground, and in that moment, I realized that every act of resistance, no matter how small, was a triumph over their oppressive silence." His words, laden with a mixture of pride and pain, encapsulated the paradox that defined the movement: every win came with a cost, and every loss, no matter how crushing, forged a new layer of determination.

In another corner of the café, Jessa, whose art had become synonymous with raw, unfiltered defiance, offered a quieter reflection. "There's a price to every revolution," she mused, her eyes distant as if recalling the long nights spent painting her defiant masterpieces. "Every time I put brush to wall, I feel the weight of what I've given up—the safety of anonymity, the comfort of routine, the warmth of a world that once understood me. But then I see the faces of those who stop to stare, who pause in their endless march of conformity, and I know that what we're doing is bigger than any personal cost. It's a transformation—a rebirth, if you will. Our sacrifices are not in vain; they are the very fuel that propels us toward a future where every human being can live in the full spectrum of truth."

Elsewhere, in the digital realm, voices continued to rise, unafraid to confront the darker aspects of their revolution. On the underground platform, heated debates raged over the merits of radical transparency versus the need for personal respite. One long, impassioned post argued that the constant exposure to unfiltered truth was a necessary crucible for growth, even if it left scars that would never fully fade. "We are forging ourselves in fire," the post declared, "and while the heat burns, it also purifies. Our wounds, though painful, are the only proof that we dared to live authentically in a world that demanded sanitised perfection." The comment sparked a flurry of responses—some commending the raw honesty, others cautioning that the unyielding march of truth might one day overwhelm the spirit.

In this complex dance of consequences and rewards, the state's reaction grew increasingly draconian. In an effort to reassert control, local authorities deployed harsher measures—unexpected raids, intensified surveillance, and a barrage of sanitised propaganda aimed at painting the rebellion as chaos incarnate. Public spaces that had once thrummed with the pulse of defiance were suddenly patrolled by armored vehicles and faceless officers in uniform. The irony was not lost on the rebels: the more the state tried to rein in the free spirit of Luminex, the more it confirmed that its vision of order was brittle and fundamentally flawed. "They're tightening the noose," one observer noted bitterly in a viral video, “but every attempt to smother us only fans the flames of our resolve.”

Yet, even amid the tightening grip of repression, there emerged moments of quiet, transformative beauty. A middle-aged woman, long disillusioned by the sterile predictability of her corporate life, found solace in the small act of rebellion—choosing to wear a handmade scarf vibrant with colors and patterns that defied all expectations. In the reflection of a rain-dappled window, she saw not the image of conformity, but a portrait of resilience—a woman who, in embracing her individuality, had reclaimed a part of her soul that she had once thought irretrievably lost. Her subtle act of defiance, shared later in a whispered conversation among like-minded friends, became a symbol of the personal revolutions that were quietly taking shape across the city.

In the aftermath of these public displays of courage, a new understanding began to take hold among the people of Luminex. The price of progress was steep, it was true—but it also bore the promise of a more vibrant, authentic existence. Each sacrifice, each painful moment of loss, was counterbalanced by a profound sense of liberation—a recognition that the freedom to be unapologetically oneself was worth every ounce of suffering endured. The rebels, in their relentless pursuit of truth, were learning that the journey toward progress was as much about internal transformation as it was about external change.

As dusk approached once more, casting long, somber shadows over the city, a quiet determination settled over the rebellion. The digital archives of personal testimonies grew richer, and the mosaic of public art continued to evolve—a living testament to the cost of revolution and the inestimable rewards it offered. The streets of Luminex, though scarred by conflict and loss, pulsed with the undeniable rhythm of a community reborn—one that had learned to cherish its imperfections and to see beauty in the struggle.

In that final moment of Part 1, as night deepened and the city braced itself for whatever consequences the state might unleash next, the rebels gathered in a small, dimly lit room. Here, amid the hushed tones and shared glances, they acknowledged the paradox at the heart of their movement: that every victory was laced with sacrifice, every beacon of hope cast a long, sometimes painful shadow. And yet, in the very act of bearing that burden, they discovered a resilience that was both humbling and exhilarating.

"We are paying a price," Lena said softly, her eyes reflecting both the pain and the promise of their journey, "but every scar is a reminder that we dared to live—and that in our brokenness, we have found a strength no state, no system, can ever crush." Her words, resonating in the silence, were a solemn vow—a promise that despite the harsh consequences, the rewards of genuine, unfiltered progress would forever be worth the cost.

And so, as the rebels prepared to face another day in a city forever altered by their defiance, the price of progress lay before them—a steep, unyielding ledger of loss and gain, etched into the very soul of Luminex. In the interplay of consequences and rewards, they had come to understand that true revolution was not measured solely by the scale of its outward victories, but by the quiet, persistent transformation that occurred within each individual soul.

As the days wore on in Luminex following the initial surge of rebellion, the cost of progress began to reveal itself in layers that were as intricate as they were painful. The city—once a gleaming symbol of controlled perfection—was now a mosaic of vibrant murals, defiant graffiti, and shattered monuments of the old order. But beneath the brilliance of these acts of transformation lay scars that ran deep, marking both the physical and emotional landscapes of its inhabitants.

In one forgotten district, where the buildings bore the weathered marks of neglect and the air was heavy with both the scent of rain and the residue of conflict, a once-thriving community center now served as a refuge for those grappling with the toll of revolution. Inside its cramped, dimly lit rooms, long after the loud protests had subsided, a quiet but profound dialogue emerged. Here, individuals shared their personal accounts of loss and sacrifice—stories that painted a picture of a progress that was both exhilarating and excruciating.

Among them was Elisa, a former boutique owner whose small shop had been the lifeblood of her community. With the advent of the rebellion, she had dared to support local artisans and independent creators, believing that a break from corporate uniformity would breathe new life into her neighborhood. But as the state's countermeasures tightened, Elisa found herself forced to shutter her doors. "I fought so hard to change the way we all lived," she murmured to a sympathetic listener, her voice quivering with a mixture of regret and resolve. "But every time I took a stand, I lost a piece of the security I once took for granted." Her words were a raw reminder that progress often demanded the sacrifice of stability—a price that weighed heavily on those who dared to dream of a freer, more authentic existence.

Across town, in a high-rise apartment with a view of the transformed urban landscape, Marcus sat alone at his desk, surrounded by the quiet hum of a world that had once seemed orderly and predictable. Once a staunch critic of the system, Marcus had become one of its most vocal proponents of change. Yet now, the ceaseless barrage of digital dissent and the constant pressure to remain on the frontlines of rebellion had begun to erode his spirit. "I used to wear my defiance like armor," he later confessed in a blog post that resonated with thousands, "but now, I feel exposed—like every word I speak is a wound waiting to reopen." His struggle was emblematic of the psychological toll that radical transformation could inflict: the relentless need to be 'on' and the emotional drain that came from living in a state of perpetual defiance.

The digital arena, once a sanctuary of unbridled freedom and raw expression, had started to reveal its own price. The underground platform—fierce, unedited, and unapologetically honest—was slowly becoming a pressure cooker of conflicting emotions. Users, emboldened by the initial surge of liberation, now found themselves caught in an endless loop of debate, introspection, and even despair. In a particularly poignant thread titled "When Freedom Burns," countless individuals shared their experiences of how constant exposure to the unvarnished truth had left them feeling emotionally raw and fatigued. One user wrote, "I thought that revealing my soul would set me free, but instead, it feels like my wounds are open for everyone to see—and sometimes, I just want them to heal in silence." The thread quickly amassed hundreds of comments, with many lamenting that the very authenticity they had once celebrated now seemed to exact a heavy toll on their mental well-being.

Yet, amid these personal and collective hardships, there emerged glimmers of reward—small, transformative moments that reminded everyone why they had chosen this perilous path. In a quiet alleyway lined with splintered wooden doors and faded posters, a group of street performers gathered to stage an impromptu act of defiant beauty. Led by a charismatic young dancer named Aisha, they transformed the grim urban backdrop into a living canvas of movement and emotion. As Aisha twirled and leaped, her body painted with vibrant hues of self-expression, onlookers found themselves captivated by a display of raw, unpolished artistry that defied the rigid constructs of their former lives. "Every movement is a rebellion," Aisha declared breathlessly between graceful spins, "every step a reclaiming of what it means to be human." The performance, recorded and shared on the underground platform, soon became a viral symbol of hope—proof that even in the midst of sacrifice, creativity could bloom, imbuing the struggle with moments of transcendent beauty.

Elsewhere, a community art project known as "The Ledger of Change" had begun to attract attention. Volunteers from various neighborhoods, ranging from former corporate workers to street vendors, had come together to document the impact of the revolution. They filled a massive wall on the side of an abandoned building with personal testimonies, photographs, and sketches—each piece a testament to both the pain and the promise of progress. One inscription read, "Every scar tells a story, and every wound is a doorway to rebirth." As passersby paused to read the heartfelt messages, many found comfort in the shared narrative of loss and renewal. The project became a living archive—a reminder that while the price of progress could be steep, it also carried the seeds of a deeper, more resilient form of beauty.

In the midst of these contrasting realities, the state's response continued to grow harsher, a reminder that the forces of order were not ready to yield without a fight. Increased patrols, surprise raids, and relentless propaganda aimed at discrediting the movement cast a long, oppressive shadow over the city. Public service announcements, replete with sanitised images of order and stability, were broadcast relentlessly, their cold, mechanical tones a stark contrast to the human stories unfolding on every street. Yet, each attempt at repression only served to underscore the cost that the establishment was willing to pay to preserve its brittle illusion of control. "They can build their walls, enforce their rules," one rebel later remarked with a dry, bitter laugh, "but every blockade only proves that our spirit—messy, wounded, and unyielding—is free."

At a dimly lit café that had become a favored haunt for those on the frontlines of the revolution, a group of rebels gathered around a battered table, their faces lit by the flickering glow of a single overhead lamp. Over steaming cups of bitter coffee, they recounted their personal losses and triumphs, trading stories of sacrifice with the same dark humor that had always been their shield against despair. "I lost someone dear last month because I couldn't stop fighting for what I believe in," confessed a wiry young man named Julian, his voice tinged with regret and resolve. "But in that loss, I found the courage to press on, to honour their memory by not compromising on the truth." His words, though heavy with sorrow, were met with nods of understanding and murmurs of solidarity—each rebel knowing that every victory on the streets came with its own cost, and that the true measure of progress was not merely in the dismantling of the old order, but in the rebuilding of lives from the ruins.

Outside, as dusk began to settle once more over a city scarred by conflict and hope, the digital and physical worlds continued to intertwine in unexpected ways. The underground platform buzzed with renewed energy as users shared fresh images and stories of the revolution's impact. A viral video montage captured a montage of faces—some defiant, some tear-streaked, all resolute—each one a living testament to the price of freedom. The post ended with a poignant message: "Every victory leaves a mark. Every gain demands a sacrifice. This is the cost of progress—but it is also its greatest reward." The video, playing over and over on shared devices, became a rallying cry—a reminder that the struggle for authenticity was both arduous and undeniably transformative.

In the midst of this maelstrom, the rebels began to see that the price of progress was not an insurmountable burden but a necessary investment in a future built on truth. It was a currency paid in tears, loss, and sleepless nights, yet it also paved the way for a society where every individual could dare to be unfiltered and whole. The personal sacrifices—lost relationships, shattered illusions, the quiet ache of solitude—were counterbalanced by the emergence of a new, vibrant community that celebrated every fracture as a point of connection and every scar as a badge of honour.

As night deepened once again, and the state's efforts to clamp down on dissent became more visible, the rebels gathered in a modest, hidden meeting room—a space carved out of an old building that had long been abandoned by those in power. In the hushed atmosphere of that room, the leaders of the movement reviewed the day's events, their faces etched with fatigue and determination. Lena, whose resolve had been tested time and again, spoke softly but firmly, "We are paying a price—one that none of us wished for—but it is the price of change. And with every sacrifice, we are forging a future that is more honest, more humane, and more resilient than the sterile world we are leaving behind." Her words, heavy with the weight of hard-won wisdom, were met with silent nods—a collective understanding that the journey ahead would be fraught with more loss, yet also filled with the promise of profound renewal.

In that moment, as the rebels prepared to disperse into the night, the dichotomy of consequences and rewards seemed to hang in the balance like a fragile, precious artifact. The price of progress was steep, but it was also the measure of their courage—a testament to the fact that true transformation was never free. And as each rebel stepped out into the rain-washed darkness, they carried with them the knowledge that every wound endured, every tear shed, and every sacrifice made was a stepping stone toward a future defined not by the absence of pain, but by the resilience to rise above it.

As days melted into nights in the turbulent city of Luminex, the early fervour of rebellion began to settle into a more somber, introspective reality. The initial burst of color and defiance that had upturned the rigid order had left behind a landscape not only scarred but also irrevocably altered. The consequences of that radical upheaval were no longer distant abstract concepts; they were tangible, etched into the very skin of the city and its inhabitants.

In the neighborhoods where once sterile, predictable routines had reigned, the weight of loss began to press down like an unyielding force. Families who had once shared a sense of quiet conformity now found themselves fractured by the choices made in the name of progress. Lena's close friend, a soft-spoken soul named Irene, had once been the picture of stability—a devoted mother and wife with a life mapped out in careful, orderly steps. But after joining the movement, Irene had lost her job and, with it, the security that had once been her anchor. Now, she wandered the same streets with eyes that shimmered with both quiet sorrow and a tentative, hopeful light. "I wanted to be free," she whispered one evening as she confided in Lena, "but I never imagined that freedom would come at the cost of everything I held dear." Her voice, heavy with regret, was a stark reminder that the price of progress was measured not only in public triumphs but in the intimate, often painful sacrifices made behind closed doors.

Even as personal losses echoed through the lives of those who dared to defy the old order, the broader repercussions of the revolution continued to unfold in unexpected ways. In one particularly affected district—a once-thriving community now overlaid with protest graffiti and defiant murals—the local economy began to buckle under the weight of incessant state crackdowns. Small businesses that had survived for decades found themselves shuttered, victims of both direct raids and the indirect consequences of a society in flux. Yet, amid the economic chaos, a new kind of marketplace emerged: an underground bazaar where artisans, street vendors, and even former corporate workers traded in ideas, art, and handmade wares that celebrated the messy reality of their existence. It was a place where the currency was not money, but authenticity—a risky, uncertain token that had the power to rebuild community even as traditional structures crumbled.

Digital spaces, too, were showing signs of wear from the constant barrage of raw, unedited content. The underground platform that had once pulsed with the raw energy of rebellion now sometimes felt like a double-edged sword. Users who had eagerly shared every unsanitised detail of their lives began to speak of "information fatigue" as the endless stream of unfiltered truths took its toll. Late at night, when the city was quiet and the glow of screens illuminated faces lined with exhaustion, debates arose about whether the relentless openness was healing or merely exposing deeper wounds. "We're burning our bridges to a safer past," one long-time user commented bitterly on a forum thread titled "Is Authenticity Exhausting?" "Every post is like a splinter in my mind." Yet even amid these confessions, there was a grudging acceptance that such scars were part of the journey—an inevitable cost for a life lived in full, unvarnished truth.

Despite these hardships, the relentless pursuit of progress began to yield rewards that were as subtle as they were profound. In a modest community garden that had sprouted in the shadow of a derelict office building, a group of neighbors—once resigned to a monotonous existence—began to cultivate a vibrant patchwork of produce and wildflowers. Tended with the same care as the underground art projects that adorned the city walls, the garden became a living metaphor for the revolution. Each seed planted was a defiant act, a deliberate gamble on the future. Neighbors, who had once whispered behind closed doors, now exchanged gardening tips and shared harvests with smiles that spoke of hope. "Even in the midst of ruin," one elderly gardener remarked, "life finds a way to flourish." The garden, though small, was a tangible reward—a reminder that amidst sacrifice and loss, new growth could emerge.

Within the heart of The Crucible—a repurposed warehouse that had become the epicenter of the rebellion—a series of intimate gatherings further revealed the dual nature of progress. In these sessions, rebels recounted their personal stories, not with the bravado of battle-hardened militants, but with the quiet vulnerability of those who had borne the full weight of change. In one such session, a young activist named Rafael, whose passionate protests had once set the streets ablaze, shared a moment of profound introspection. "I used to think that my defiance was my only shield," he admitted, his voice soft yet laden with raw emotion, "but now I see that vulnerability—acknowledging our fears, our losses—is what truly makes us resilient. Every wound is a record of our struggle, and every scar a reminder that we dared to be human." His words were met with nods and murmurs of agreement—a collective acknowledgment that the transformation being wrought in Luminex was as much about internal revolution as it was about external change.

Helena, who had guided many through the labyrinth of moral philosophy, began to host quiet, reflective discussions on the nature of sacrifice and reward. In one session held in a refurbished classroom at a community center, she posed a simple yet piercing question: "What is the cost of progress?" The room fell into a contemplative silence as participants, from hardened rebels to disillusioned citizens, wrestled with the question. Some spoke of the tangible losses—jobs, relationships, a sense of security—while others lamented the intangible, such as the erosion of innocence and the persistent ache of uncertainty. Yet, as the discussion unfolded, a unifying theme emerged: that the price of progress was not merely a series of losses, but also the foundation for a richer, more authentic future. "Every sacrifice," one elderly woman asserted, "is an investment in a world where our true selves can finally emerge from the shadows." Her words, echoing through the room, encapsulated the paradox at the heart of the revolution: that pain and reward were inseparable partners in the dance of change.

Back on the streets, the visual reminders of this duality became more frequent. A once-sterile alleyway was transformed into a mural that depicted a figure carrying a heavy burden—a giant, shadowy mass that represented the weight of sacrifice—yet the figure's determined eyes shone with hope and defiance. The inscription below read, "Every burden carried is a step toward freedom." Such images resonated deeply with passersby, who found in them both a mirror of their own struggles and a beacon guiding them toward a future where the sacrifices of today would yield the rewards of tomorrow.

Meanwhile, in the digital arena, discussions about the price of progress began to shape the collective narrative. A series of live-streamed panel discussions titled "The Ledger of Sacrifice" attracted thousands of viewers. Moderated by veterans of the rebellion, these sessions featured raw, unfiltered accounts of the personal costs of defiance alongside optimistic visions for the future. Participants debated fiercely, their exchanges filled with dark humor and unyielding honesty. One panelist, a disillusioned former executive, noted, "I lost everything I once thought was important—but in that loss, I discovered what truly matters. It's a bitter lesson, but it's a lesson nonetheless." His words, delivered with a mix of regret and quiet pride, served as a stark reminder that progress was a double-edged sword—a tool for both destruction and creation.

As the twilight deepened, the repercussions of the state's renewed repressive measures became increasingly evident. In one sector of the city, a series of raids led to the arrest of several outspoken community organizers. Their detentions, widely circulated on the underground platform, sparked a wave of solidarity and indignation. Crowds gathered outside police stations, chanting slogans that denounced the cruelty of those in power. Although these confrontations were marred by the fear and chaos inherent in any violent response, they also revealed the unbreakable spirit of the people of Luminex—a spirit that refused to be cowed by even the most brutal tactics.

Yet, amid the turmoil, there were moments of unexpected tenderness—a reminder that progress, with all its heavy costs, also nurtured a new kind of connection among people. In a modest apartment block that had once been a symbol of isolation, neighbors began organizing small support groups. Over shared meals and long conversations in the glow of flickering streetlights, individuals who had suffered personal losses found solace in each other's stories. They discovered that in the shared language of pain, there was also the potential for healing—a chance to rebuild bonds that had been severed by the relentless pace of change. One elderly man, his voice soft with emotion, confided, "I've lost so much—my job, my friends, my old self—but in this struggle, I've found something more precious: a community that understands the price we pay and the rewards we earn, however slowly." His words, whispered in the quiet intimacy of a newly formed circle of friends, echoed the universal truth that progress was not a solitary endeavor but a collective journey, marked by both sacrifice and profound, unexpected connection.

In the midst of this evolving landscape of loss and hope, the rebels and the citizens of Luminex gradually began to see that the price of progress was not a burden to be resented but a testament to their commitment to a deeper truth. The daily struggles, the heartbreak of personal sacrifice, and the relentless state of unrest all converged to forge a new understanding—a realization that every wound, every tear, every moment of despair was the raw material from which a more vibrant, authentic future could be built.

As the night waned and the first light of a new day began to crest the horizon, the city stood as a living ledger of its own transformation. Every scar on its buildings, every defiant slogan painted on its walls, bore witness to the heavy cost of change. And while the state's attempts to quash the rebellion continued to inflict pain, they also inadvertently fortified the resolve of those who had embraced the path of progress.

In the quiet aftermath of the day's struggles, as individual hearts beat in unison with the collective rhythm of the revolution, a new mantra began to take shape in the minds of the people: that the true measure of progress was not found in the absence of loss, but in the resilience to rise from those very losses. For every personal sacrifice, there was a corresponding reward—a growth in wisdom, a deeper sense of community, a reclamation of one's true self. And in this ongoing ledger of pain and triumph, Luminex was gradually learning to value the scars as much as the victories.

Night fell over Luminex with a quiet, almost mournful finality. The chaos of recent days had begun to settle into a heavy, reflective silence—a silence filled with the echoes of both victory and loss. The city's streets, once alive with the electric pulse of rebellion, now bore scars like a patient's well-worn skin, each crack a reminder of sacrifices made in the name of progress.

In a small, dimly lit room tucked away in an old building that had once housed the offices of a defunct corporation, a final gathering of the core rebels took place. The air was thick with the hum of low conversation and the soft clatter of old keyboards, as Lena, Marcus, Jessa, Helena, and a handful of their closest allies sat in a rough circle. The mood was somber—no longer solely fueled by the adrenaline of defiance, but now tempered by the weight of what had been lost along the way.

Lena, her face lined with fatigue and determination, began softly. "We knew this wouldn't be easy," she said, her voice steady but laced with a hint of sorrow. "We set out to tear down the walls of conformity, to reclaim our freedom. But every act of rebellion, every time we risked everything, came with a price we could never fully predict." She paused, looking around at the others whose eyes shone with shared memories of hardship. "I see it in our faces—the deep lines, the shadows behind our smiles. We have paid dearly."

Marcus, who had once been the biting cynic and the fierce herald of the revolution, now spoke with an uncharacteristic tenderness. "Every scar tells a story," he murmured. "I remember a protest we held on a rainy night when we thought we could change the world in a single moment. In that moment, I felt invincible. But now, in the quiet after the storm, I feel every bruise, every tear, as a reminder that nothing comes without cost. I lost friends... sometimes even a piece of who I was before." His voice faltered slightly, betraying the heavy toll of constant struggle.

Across the room, Jessa traced a finger over a fresh mark on the wall—a mural that had been defaced by state agents only a few days earlier. "My art was always my rebellion," she said, her tone softening from its usual fierce edge. "When I painted those slogans and images, I believed I was immortalising our defiance. But I also realised that every stroke was a sacrifice—of time, of safety, of a piece of myself that I can never get back." Her eyes shimmered with unshed tears as she continued, "Yet, when I see someone stop in their tracks to look at that mural, to feel even a fraction of what I felt, I know it wasn't all in vain."

Helena, ever the thoughtful mediator and former professor, reflected on the broader meaning of their revolution. "Progress is a paradox," she said, her voice quiet but resolute. "We are rewriting history not by erasing the past, but by embracing it—the pain, the mistakes, the beauty of imperfection. It is in our wounds that we find the true measure of our resilience. Each loss, every heartbreak, is also a lesson. And in those lessons, there is hope, however faint."

Outside the meeting room, the city itself bore the indelible imprint of their struggle. In a narrow alley, a weathered mural depicted a solitary figure, head bowed yet with eyes lifted toward a sliver of light piercing through dark clouds. The inscription beneath read, "From every wound, we rise." Passersby slowed their hurried steps, many pausing to trace the intricate lines of defiance that had now become a part of Luminex's evolving identity. The mural was a silent testament—a visual ledger of all that had been sacrificed and all that had been gained.

Elsewhere, the underground digital platform buzzed with a new kind of dialogue. In threads titled "The Cost of Truth" and "Our Silent Wounds," users shared intimate stories of personal sacrifice. One particularly poignant post came from a young woman who recounted the loss of a long-time friend, taken away by the pressures of a system that demanded constant vigilance and rebellion. "I miss the laughter we once shared," she wrote, "and the simple moments when we weren't forced to fight. But in our shared grief, I also find a strange strength—a reminder that our struggle is not just for ourselves, but for the hope that we can build a better world from these very ashes." Comments poured in with empathy and solidarity, a digital chorus mourning the heavy price of their freedom while also celebrating the bonds forged in the crucible of resistance.

In the heart of one of the transformed neighbourhoods, the community garden—once an underground experiment—continued to thrive as a living symbol of renewal. Neighbours tended to their plots with quiet diligence, their faces etched with the hardships of the past but also illuminated by the hope of new beginnings. A weathered sign at the garden's entrance read, "Every seed of change grows from the soil of sacrifice." Here, amid the fragrant scent of earth and the gentle murmur of conversation, people found solace in the tangible evidence that even after all the pain, life could blossom in unexpected ways.

At The Crucible, the epicentre of the cultural revolution, a final public event was organised—a night of remembrance and celebration. On a makeshift stage under a canopy of string lights, a diverse group of citizens gathered to honour both the losses and the victories of their shared journey. Among them were poets, musicians, and everyday people who had been touched by the rebellion. A soft melody filled the air as a young violinist played a haunting tune that seemed to capture both the sorrow and the beauty of their collective experience.

One by one, speakers took the stage. An elderly man, whose decades of conformity had given way to a late-life awakening, spoke of his regret for lost time but also of the priceless moments of authentic connection he had found in the revolution's wake. "I have seen the worst and the best of what it means to be human," he said, his voice cracking with emotion. "The price we pay is steep, but every sacrifice has taught us the value of a life lived without pretence. We are wounded, yes—but we are also whole."

A young woman, her face streaked with tears and illuminated by the soft glow of stage lights, recited a poem that had quickly become a rallying cry among the rebels. "Our wounds are our stories," she intoned, "etched deep into our hearts as reminders of what we have endured, and what we dare to reclaim. Each tear is a tribute to our journey—a testament to the courage it takes to leave behind the safety of the known for the uncertainty of a better tomorrow." Her words, tender yet fierce, resonated with every listener, drawing a collective, tearful applause that was both a celebration and a mourning.

By the time the event drew to a close, the mood had shifted from the raw intensity of battle to a reflective, almost melancholic hope. The rebels and citizens of Luminex had come to see that the cost of progress was a mosaic of loss and gain—a ledger where every heartbreak was balanced by a moment of unexpected beauty. The price they had paid was not a tally of defeats, but a collection of hard-won victories that had reshaped their understanding of what it meant to live authentically.

In the quiet that followed the celebration, as people slowly dispersed into the cool night, Lena returned once more to her rooftop—a solitary figure against the sprawling, scarred cityscape. The neon lights below glowed softly, each flicker a reminder of the lives that had been touched, the sacrifices made, and the resilience that now defined Luminex. She closed her eyes and allowed herself a moment of vulnerability—a silent, intimate acknowledgment of the burdens she bore. "We have given so much," she whispered into the night, “and yet in every loss, there is a spark of hope. Our scars, though painful, are the emblems of our strength. They tell the story of who we were, who we are, and who we can become.”

In that quiet solitude, the full weight of the revolution pressed upon her—a bittersweet mixture of regret and pride, sorrow and resolve. Lena knew that the battle was far from over; that every step forward would continue to demand sacrifices. But in that acceptance, she found a deep, emotional wellspring of determination. The price of progress was steep, but it was the very currency of their rebirth—a testament to the fact that the journey toward true freedom was measured not in the absence of pain, but in the courage to rise again after every fall.

And so, as the first light of dawn began to soften the dark edges of the night, Luminex awoke not as a city unscarred, but as a living, breathing testament to the cost—and the reward—of progress. The revolution had left its mark on every street, every soul, and every whispered conversation. In the interplay of consequences and rewards, the people of Luminex had learned that their true strength lay in their ability to endure, to adapt, and to find beauty even in the most painful of changes.

In that fragile, hopeful morning, as Lena joined others in the early quiet of the city—neighbours tending to gardens, shopkeepers opening doors, and families sharing simple smiles—a new chapter began. It was a chapter that acknowledged the heavy price they had paid and celebrated the unyielding resilience that had carried them through. The ledger of progress, though marked by loss and sorrow, was also illuminated by the light of rebirth and renewal—a light that promised that, in every sacrifice, there was a seed of a better, truer future.

CHAPTER NINE

Rewriting the Moral Code

In the grim tapestry of Luminex's past, morality had long been a sterile, bureaucratic decree—a set of rules etched in stone by those who feared the unruly nature of the human spirit. The establishment prided itself on a moral code so meticulously curated that it left little room for spontaneity, creativity, or the messy beauty of genuine life. It was a code that, in its quest for order, reduced every human nuance to a checkbox on an endless form, a series of predetermined virtues and vices meant to control behaviour rather than celebrate individuality.

How laughable, one might have thought, to insist that true morality could be distilled into neat, immutable lines. The same forces that championed "integrity" and "discipline" had long since proven themselves incapable of acknowledging the very flaws that made humanity vibrant. They preached honesty while cloaking themselves in hypocrisy, demanded conformity while suppressing dissent, and sanctified mediocrity while condemning the passion of the imperfect. With every cold, calculated edict, the old moral code revealed its inherent absurdity—a relic of a bygone era that had no place in a city that was quickly learning to revel in its own beautifully chaotic truth.

And yet, even as the state's moral dogma crumbled under the weight of its own contradictions, there remained an undercurrent of dark humour—a sardonic acknowledgment that, for all its pomp and solemnity, the old code was nothing more than a carefully constructed farce. In the crowded corridors of government buildings, officials would chuckle quietly behind closed doors at the irony of their own declarations. "Virtue," one bureaucrat muttered under his breath during a particularly tedious meeting, "is nothing more than a luxury we can't afford in a world that demands survival." Such remarks, though whispered and hidden from the public eye, encapsulated the pervasive sense of disillusionment that had seeped into the very foundations of the city.

In the wake of the revolution that had upended Luminex, the remnants of that old moral order clashed violently with a new, emerging consciousness. On every street corner and in every shadowed alley, people were beginning to question the rigid dichotomies of right and wrong. What had once been cast as sin was now celebrated as the wellspring of creativity; what was once deemed virtuous was seen as a sterile façade designed to stifle genuine emotion. The rebels had taken these contradictions and transformed them into the fuel for a new kind of morality—a morality that was as fluid, complex, and human as the people who embraced it.

In a cramped underground café, where the stale aroma of burnt coffee mixed with the sharp tang of defiance, a small group of rebels gathered for an informal discussion on what the future might hold. The conversation was as unpredictable as the people around the table, oscillating between biting sarcasm and tentative hope. "Our old moral code," one participant scoffed, swirling the remnants of his cheap whiskey in a chipped glass, "was a patchwork of empty promises. It told us to be honest, but only when it was convenient. It preached compassion, but only for those who fit neatly into its approved categories. We were expected to be paragons of virtue while the system itself wallowed in hypocrisy." His words drew a ripple of agreement from those gathered, their laughter laced with a bitter understanding of how the old order had betrayed its own ideals.

Across the table, a young woman with ink-stained fingers and a gaze that flickered between defiance and longing offered her perspective. "Maybe," she began slowly, "it's time we rewrite what morality means. Not as a set of rigid rules, but as a living, breathing code that grows and changes with us. I'm tired of a morality that punishes me for my flaws instead of celebrating them. What if our vices—the impulses that once made us outcasts—are not the enemy at all, but the catalyst for a deeper, more honest virtue?" Her voice, quiet but resolute, cut through the room like a spark in the darkness. The notion, radical in its simplicity, resonated deeply with the rebels. They had long been told that their wild impulses, their mistakes, were sins to be expunged. Yet, in the raw reality of their experiences, they began to see that these very imperfections were what gave life its texture and meaning.

That afternoon, as rain dripped in a steady cadence over the city's neon-soaked streets, the mood among the rebels shifted imperceptibly. The dark sarcasm that had once dominated every conversation now began to yield to something more nuanced—a revolutionary spark that hinted at the possibility of forging a new moral code. In the graffiti-scarred back alleys of Luminex, slogans that once derided the old order now morphed into hopeful declarations: "Our Flaws, Our Freedom" and "Imperfection Is the New Virtue." These words, scrawled hastily on crumbling walls, were more than just rebellious taglines; they were a manifesto of transformation—a call to redefine what it meant to be truly human in a world that had long worshipped superficial perfection.

At The Crucible, the cultural epicentre of the revolution, an experimental art installation was unveiled. The piece, titled "The Moral Mosaic," was a sprawling canvas composed of thousands of fragments—each piece a raw photograph of everyday life in Luminex, capturing moments of joy, despair, rebellion, and tenderness. The fragments, arranged haphazardly yet intentionally, formed an image that was both chaotic and beautiful—a human face emerging from the collage, its features rough-hewn and imperfect, yet undeniably real. As onlookers gathered, murmuring in awe, the curator—a veteran of the movement known only as Rafi—stepped forward and addressed the crowd. "This," he declared, his voice trembling with a mixture of pride and sorrow, "is our new moral code. It is not a prescription, but a revelation—a reminder that every scar, every broken piece, and every burst of defiance is a part of the whole. Our morality is not fixed; it is as dynamic, as fluid, as the very life that courses through our veins."

The crowd's reaction was electric—a blend of applause and quiet contemplation that echoed the growing realisation that the old moral paradigms were crumbling under the weight of their own contradictions. Here, in the heart of a city reborn through rebellion, the seeds of a new ethical vision were being sown—a vision that embraced the full spectrum of human experience, from the darkest impulses to the most luminous acts of compassion.

As dusk approached and the day's reflective energy began to merge with the encroaching night, the rebels dispersed into the city, each carrying with them the embers of this revolutionary idea. In the quiet aftermath, as neon lights flickered over rain-slicked pavements, individual acts of defiance took on new meaning. A street vendor, who had once sold identical, sanitised snacks to obedient commuters, began offering small, handmade treats—each one a unique blend of flavours, unpredictable and boldly different from the standard fare. A group of office workers, inspired by the discussions at the café, started an impromptu "Moral Hour" during lunch breaks, where they shared stories of personal failure and unexpected redemption—a space where vulnerability was not a weakness, but a strength to be celebrated.

Even the digital landscape began to transform as users on the underground platform started sharing not only their revolutionary outcries but also their heartfelt confessions. A thread titled "Rewriting My Code" became a sanctuary for those who had found themselves caught between the dictates of an old, repressive morality and the burgeoning desire for a more authentic way of living. In that thread, a once-proud lawyer detailed how his rigid adherence to outdated principles had alienated him from the very essence of life, and how, in embracing his contradictions, he had discovered a depth of empathy and creativity he never knew existed. His story, like so many others, resonated deeply—its raw, unvarnished truth igniting a spark of hope in others who were struggling to reconcile their inner conflicts.

In a quiet residential street, illuminated by the soft glow of street-lamps and the persistent patter of rain, an elderly neighbour named Agnes stepped out onto her porch. For decades, she had lived by the strict moral codes that her generation held dear, believing them to be the only path to a dignified life. But in recent months, Agnes had begun to notice subtle changes around her—the sound of laughter spilling from a once-silent community centre, the sight of colourful art brightening the drab walls of her block, and the gentle, unspoken bonds forming among neighbours who dared to break free of convention. As she watched a group of teenagers sharing secret smiles and spontaneous hugs, Agnes felt a stirring of something unfamiliar—a longing for a life that embraced the full range of emotion, both the bittersweet and the beautiful. "Maybe there's more to life than the rigid rules I once knew," she whispered to herself, a tentative smile emerging from beneath a lifetime of stern expression.

That evening, as the sky darkened and the city's pulse shifted into a more introspective rhythm, a public forum was organised at a repurposed theatre—a place that had once hosted sterile performances of classical plays but was now a venue for raw, revolutionary dialogue. The forum, aptly titled "Moral Reclamation," drew a diverse crowd: young activists with faces alight with defiant hope, middle-aged citizens quietly questioning the status quo, and even a few disillusioned former enforcers of the old regime. On stage, Helena, whose wisdom had guided many through the labyrinth of moral ambiguity, addressed the assembly. "For too long," she began, her voice firm yet imbued with gentle compassion, "we have allowed an outdated moral code—one that demanded perfection and punished the beautiful mess of our humanity—to dictate our lives. Today, we stand at the threshold of a new era—a time to reclaim our true selves, not by rejecting morality altogether, but by rewriting it. Let us forge a code that honours both our strength and our fragility, our defiance and our compassion."

Her words, once delivered with dark sarcasm and now resonating with revolutionary clarity, stirred the crowd into a unified, hopeful murmur.

As the forum continued, speakers shared personal testimonies of transformation—stories of how breaking free from the oppressive molds of the past had led them to rediscover the vibrant, multifaceted nature of their humanity. Each narrative was a testament to the power of self-reclamation—a declaration that morality need not be a set of immutable commandments, but a living, evolving dialogue between the heart and the mind. "We are not defined by the rigid labels of 'good' and 'evil,'" one speaker proclaimed, his eyes glistening with unshed tears. "We are defined by our capacity to learn, to adapt, and to love even in our brokenness." The audience, moved by the raw sincerity of these confessions, responded with applause that was both celebratory and cathartic—a collective exhale of years spent suppressing the truth of who they were.

By the close of the forum, a palpable shift had occurred. The dark, sarcastic critiques of the old moral code had given way to a budding revolutionary spirit—a spirit that believed in the possibility of a morality rewritten in the ink of authenticity and shared struggle. The forum ended with a call to action: a rally scheduled for the following week, where citizens were invited to come together and craft a new moral manifesto—a document that would capture the lessons learned from their collective journey and serve as a foundation for a society that valued the full spectrum of human experience.

As the crowd dispersed into the cool night, the reverberations of Helena's words lingered in the air—a promise that the convergence of vice and virtue was not merely a theoretical exercise, but a tangible, transformative force. In that moment, as the neon lights of Luminex flickered against the dark sky, every soul present felt the stirrings of revolution—a realisation that the time had come to reclaim not only their freedom but the very meaning of what it meant to be moral.

In the wake of the public forum and the stirring testimonies that had rocked the gathered crowd, Luminex began to feel the tremors of a shift not only in its political landscape but also in its very ethical foundation. The echoes of Helena's words and the collective outpouring of personal revelations rippled outward, weaving their way through the city's narrow streets and expansive digital networks. Now, as the day unfolded, those same dark, biting critiques of the old order were slowly giving way to a renewed, almost tangible energy—a revolution in thought that promised a reimagining of what it meant to be moral.

In a quiet, dimly lit room tucked away behind an aging brick building in one of the city's less patrolled districts, a diverse group of citizens gathered in a secret meeting that would serve as a crucible for this evolving dialogue. The room was modest—a collection of mismatched chairs and a battered whiteboard where ideas could be scrawled in haste. Here, individuals from all walks of life—former bureaucrats disillusioned by years of conformity, street artists whose work had long defied societal expectations, and even skeptical students hungry for a deeper meaning—sat together to engage in a conversation that was as raw as it was hopeful.

At the head of the table, a man named Victor, whose once razor-sharp sarcasm had earned him a reputation as a fearless critic of the old code, took a deep breath. "We've spent so long mocking a system that told us what was right and what was wrong," he began, his tone still tinged with that characteristic dry humour. "But what if, instead of just tearing down that system, we were bold enough to rebuild it from the ground up? Not with sterile rules and empty virtues, but with something that reflects who we really are—our flaws, our passions, our chaos, and yes, even our moments of tenderness." His words hung in the air, a subtle pivot from ridicule to genuine possibility.

As murmurs of agreement rippled around the table, a young woman named Suri—whose eyes sparkled with both mischief and a deep-seated yearning for change—picked up the conversation. "I've always been told that my impulsiveness, my 'reckless' behaviour, is a vice," she said, her voice soft but resolute. "But I've come to realise that those very impulses are what make me, me. They're the sparks that ignite creativity and drive change. Instead of denying that side of us, maybe it's time we embrace it and redefine it as a kind of virtue—a necessary ingredient in the recipe for progress." Her words, part confession and part manifesto, struck a chord among those present. They began to see that the same qualities once scorned as immoral might, in the context of an evolving society, be recast as essential to our humanity.

Outside the secret meeting, the city itself was a canvas for this new discourse. In the fading light of a late afternoon, a mural had been unveiled on a once-forgotten wall in a busy district. The piece was a bold, intricate work that juxtaposed images of old moral symbols—scales of justice, ancient scrolls, and stern, classical busts—with the unruly, vibrant strokes of contemporary graffiti. In the centre, large, fluid letters declared: "Morality Reborn." The mural was both an act of defiance and a hopeful invitation; it invited viewers to question the old, rigid definitions and consider the possibility of a living, breathing moral code that could adapt to the complexities of modern life.

Digital spaces, too, played their part in this transformation. The underground platform that had once been a hotbed of raw, unfiltered dissent now buzzed with thoughtful debates and collaborative projects. A new hashtag—#CodeRewritten—began to trend among users, who posted essays, poems, and even short films exploring what a reimagined morality might look like. One viral video, a poignant montage of everyday moments captured on shaky smartphone footage, contrasted scenes of corporate monotony with those of vibrant, spontaneous street celebrations. The video ended with a message: "It's time to rewrite our moral code—not as a set of rigid prescriptions, but as a reflection of our shared, messy humanity." The digital response was overwhelming: thousands of comments, likes, and shares, as users from all corners of Luminex and beyond joined in a collective rethinking of values.

As dusk settled into the cool embrace of early evening, the group in the secret meeting reconvened to refine their ideas. Victor stood before the whiteboard, marker in hand, and began to sketch out a tentative framework—a set of principles that might form the foundation of a new moral code. "Let's start with the idea that our morality should be fluid," he wrote, his handwriting bold and determined. "It must evolve with us, incorporate our failures as well as our triumphs, and celebrate the messy interplay between what we once called vice and what we used to label virtue." His colleagues nodded, adding their own thoughts: that authenticity, empathy, and resilience must be at the core of this new code; that compassion should not be measured by the ability to conform but by the courage to be imperfect; that creativity—unfettered by outdated norms—was not just desirable but essential.

Suri, with a fervour that belied her youth, added, "We need a code that understands that the impulse to rebel isn't inherently immoral. That sometimes, the very act of defiance is the purest form of honesty we can offer to ourselves and to the world." Her suggestion sparked an animated discussion about the need to dismantle binary thinking—a dichotomy of good versus evil that had long suffocated the human spirit. "What if we replace that binary with a spectrum?" suggested an older participant, his voice measured with the wisdom of years spent in quiet observation. "A spectrum that acknowledges every shade of our experience—from the darkest impulses to the brightest acts of kindness—is what truly defines us."

Outside, the murmuring voices of revolution had grown into a quiet roar as the city's inhabitants began to take tentative steps toward this new vision. In the corridors of once-sterile government buildings, whispers of change circulated alongside the usual guarded glances. Even those who had once been the staunch defenders of the old order found themselves pausing in quiet reflection when confronted with the vibrant expressions of individuality that now adorned the city's walls.

As the secret meeting drew to a close, the group decided to take their evolving framework into the public arena. They planned to organise a series of "Moral Workshops" in community centers and public parks—spaces where citizens could come together to discuss, debate, and ultimately help draft a collective moral manifesto. The idea was revolutionary in its inclusiveness: rather than imposing a top-down decree, the new moral code would be built from the ground up, shaped by the diverse voices and experiences of the people of Luminex. It was a bold experiment—one that acknowledged that while the old code had been suffocating, the process of crafting a new one would be messy, challenging, and, above all, profoundly human.

In the days that followed, the planning for these workshops took on a life of its own. Flyers began to appear in coffee shops, on bulletin boards, and even in digital spaces—a call to join the conversation, to help shape a future that celebrated the entirety of one's experience. The hashtag #RecodeLuminex started to trend among the underground community, with people sharing their ideas for a moral code that would be as dynamic and multifaceted as the lives they led. Stories poured in from across the city: a construction worker described how he had learned to see his dangerous, daily risks as acts of survival that carried their own dignity; a young mother shared how embracing her imperfections had transformed her relationship with her children, teaching them that love was not conditional on flawlessness; a retired teacher recalled how questioning long-held moral dogmas had rekindled her passion for learning and inspired her to start a new curriculum that celebrated creative thinking.

Back in the secret meeting room, as the group prepared to disband for the evening, Victor gathered the papers and sketches that now formed the tentative outline of their new moral framework. "We're at the beginning of something truly radical," he said, his voice low but filled with a stirring conviction. "This isn't about rejecting morality—it's about reclaiming it, reshaping it to reflect our reality. We've seen the failures of the old code, and we've experienced the painful costs of progress. Now, it's time to harness that pain, to let it fuel a future that's not defined by fear or conformity, but by the full, vibrant spectrum of who we are." His words, echoing in the quiet room, were both a challenge and an invitation—a call for every person who had ever felt stifled by rigid rules to stand up and contribute to a revolution of the soul.

As twilight faded into a gentle, hopeful darkness, the seeds of this new moral vision began to take root in the hearts of the rebels and, increasingly, in the wider community. The convergence of vice and virtue was no longer a theoretical possibility; it was becoming a living, breathing reality—a process that would require time, patience, and relentless determination to nurture. Yet, for the first time in a long while, there was a palpable sense of possibility—a belief that the old, suffocating definitions of morality could be dismantled and rebuilt into something that celebrated every facet of the human experience.

In the quiet hours before midnight, as the group dispersed into the cool, reflective night, each person carried with them the embers of a new revolution—a quiet, powerful determination to rewrite the moral code of their city. They knew that the road ahead would be fraught with challenges and that many would resist this radical reimagining. But within those very challenges lay the promise of a future where truth was not measured by rigid conformity, but by the courage to embrace life in all its imperfect, unpredictable glory.

And so, as the neon glow of Luminex mingled with the soft luminescence of a breaking dawn, the transformation was underway—a metamorphosis not just of buildings and streets, but of hearts and minds. In that delicate, transitional space, the old moral code, with all its hypocrisy and rigidity, began to crumble, replaced by a new ethic born from the union of defiant vice and nurturing virtue—a code that promised to honour every story, every struggle, every unfiltered moment of life.

In the waning hours of a long, turbulent day in Luminex, when the scars of rebellion shimmered under the soft glow of neon and dawn's first light, the remnants of the old moral order seemed to crumble like brittle ruins. For too long, the city had been ruled by an archaic code—an edict of pristine, sterile values that had served only to stifle the raw, untamed beauty of human existence. But now, as the collective consciousness of Luminex pulsed with the energy of transformation, the time had come to cast aside that rigid past and forge a new future from the ashes of outdated dogma.

On a quiet rooftop overlooking the transformed urban landscape, Lena stood with her eyes fixed on the horizon. The city below was no longer the uniform, controlled tableau it once had been. Instead, every wall, every street, every small act of defiance had contributed to a living mosaic—a testament to the sacrifices and triumphs of a people determined to reclaim their identity. Lena's heart, which had borne the weight of countless losses and sleepless nights, now beat with the steady, insistent rhythm of hope. "We are more than the sum of our scars," she thought, her inner voice no longer tinged with bitter sarcasm but with resolute conviction. "Every wound, every painful memory, is a reminder of the price we've paid—and the promise we now hold."

Across the city, the revolution was reaching into every hidden corner. In a bustling community centre that had been repurposed into a forum for change, citizens of all ages gathered for what was being called "The New Covenant." Here, the idea was simple yet radical: to come together and collaboratively draft a moral manifesto that reflected the full, unpredictable spectrum of their lives. The participants were an unlikely mix—former enforcers of the old system, tired bureaucrats, street artists, poets, and everyday people whose lives had been forever altered by the struggle for authenticity. They came with bruised hearts and determined spirits, ready to break free from the binary notions of sin and sanctity.

At the front of the packed hall, Helena stepped onto a makeshift stage. Her once academic tone had softened into something warmer, more human, as she addressed the crowd. "For decades, we were fed a narrow narrative—a morality defined by rigid rules and false dichotomies," she began. "But our journey has shown us that our true strength lies not in pretending to be flawless, but in embracing our messiness, our contradictions. Today, we gather to rewrite the moral code—a code that honours our struggles, celebrates our resilience, and accepts that the path to progress is paved with both vice and virtue." Her words, resonant and unburdened by cynicism, sparked an immediate, electric response from the audience—a murmur of hope that rippled through the room like a warm breeze.

In that same forum, a young poet named Suri took the stage next. Her eyes shone with a fierce vulnerability as she recited lines that captured the paradox of human imperfection. "We once believed that virtue meant perfection," she intoned, "but I now see that our beauty lies in the cracks. It is in our errors, in our rebellions, that we discover who we truly are. Let our flaws be the ink with which we write a new moral story—a story that honours both the fire of our defiance and the tenderness of our compassion." The audience sat spellbound, the air heavy with the promise of transformation. In that moment, the old moral code began to dissolve, replaced by a nascent, inclusive vision that celebrated every facet of the human spirit.

Outside the community centre, the streets of Luminex were alive with the tangible echoes of this emerging new ethos. In the financial district—once a bastion of sterile order—digital billboards now cycled through images of everyday people: a construction worker smiling despite his calloused hands, an elderly woman laughing amid the graffiti-covered walls of her building, and groups of young activists joining hands in spontaneous acts of solidarity. Each image was accompanied by a simple, powerful message: "Reclaim Your Truth," "Embrace Every Shade of You," "Our Strength Lies in Our Imperfections." These messages, bold and unpolished, captured the revolutionary spirit that was now permeating the city.

The digital realm, too, had become a crucible for this reborn morality. The underground platform that had once been a battlefield of raw, unfiltered emotion now served as a collective studio where people from every walk of life could contribute to the conversation. Threads titled "Our New Covenant" and "Rewriting the Code" were filled with collaborative essays, digital art, and personal testimonies. A viral video, featuring a montage of faces from across Luminex—each sharing a brief statement about the complexity of their inner worlds—ended with the words, "We Are Whole Because We Are Human." The comments that followed were not the cacophonous rants of previous days; they were thoughtful, introspective reflections, a chorus of voices daring to imagine a future where morality was as multifaceted as the people it was meant to serve.

In a small, repurposed studio near The Crucible, a group of artists and philosophers gathered to brainstorm ideas for the new moral manifesto. Their workspace was cluttered with sketches, calligraphy, and fragments of conversation scribbled on scraps of paper. Victor, whose earlier sardonic critiques had softened into a measured passion, began outlining the principles that might guide this new code. "We need to start with the idea that morality isn't static," he said, his hand steady as he drew sweeping lines on a whiteboard. "It must evolve—reflecting the dynamic interplay between our light and dark sides. We must honour our capacity to rebel, to err, and to grow. Let our code be a living document, updated by each of us as we learn from our experiences." His voice, once laced with irony, now carried the weight of sincere conviction, and every nod from his peers confirmed that they were ready to break free from the chains of an antiquated system.

Over the next several days, plans for a series of public "Moral Workshops" began to take shape. These workshops were to be held in parks, community centers, and even on the streets—spaces where citizens could come together to share their stories, debate ideas, and collaboratively draft the blueprint for a new moral order. Flyers bearing the bold title "Recode Luminex" were posted in unexpected places—a quiet protest against the old guard's insistence on order. The call was simple: join us in a revolution of ethics, where every voice matters, and every truth, no matter how raw, contributes to our collective humanity.

As these initiatives gained traction, the tone across the city began to shift noticeably. The harsh, biting sarcasm of the past was gradually replaced by a more nuanced, heartfelt discourse. Conversations that once centered solely on dismantling the old code now pivoted to envisioning what the new code could be. In the corridors of government buildings and corporate offices, the suppressed murmurs of discontent grew louder—not as cries of anger, but as calls for a more compassionate, honest framework for living. Even those who had once been stalwart defenders of the status quo started to question their own convictions. In hushed tones, they admitted that the rigid, black-and-white morality they had upheld for so long had left little room for the beautiful complexities of life.

The revolution in Luminex was, at its core, a transformation of identity—a reclaiming of what it meant to be truly human. And as the idea of rewriting the moral code took hold, there emerged a powerful sense of unity among the people. The lines that had once divided society—between rebel and conformist, between vice and virtue—began to blur into insignificance. Instead, a new vision emerged: one in which morality was not a set of prescriptions imposed from above, but a shared, evolving narrative crafted by the lived experiences of every individual.

By the time the first of the Moral Workshops was held in a sunlit public park, a palpable sense of anticipation filled the air. Citizens gathered in small groups on picnic blankets, beneath trees whose leaves whispered secrets of change. Facilitators—trained in the art of open dialogue and genuine listening—guided discussions that allowed participants to explore their own definitions of right and wrong. One group, consisting of elderly residents and spirited young activists alike, debated the merits of forgiveness versus accountability. "I believe," one participant said softly, "that our moral code should allow for redemption, that even the gravest missteps can lead to growth if we're given the chance to learn and change." Another countered, "But we must also remember that actions have consequences; our code must not be an excuse for perpetual chaos." The conversation was neither easy nor tidy, but it was honest—a microcosm of the new, inclusive morality that was beginning to emerge.

At the same time, digital conversations on the underground platform grew richer and more collaborative. People shared drafts of their ideas, debated the merits of different principles, and even organised virtual workshops that connected citizens from disparate parts of Luminex. The hashtag #RecodeLuminex became a symbol of this evolving movement—a rallying cry that encapsulated the belief that morality, like society, must be constantly rewritten to reflect the realities of human existence.

In one particularly moving online exchange, a former corporate executive, whose life had been transformed by the revolution, wrote, "I spent years in a world of sterile rules and empty metrics. Now, I see that true virtue lies in the willingness to be imperfect, to risk failure in the pursuit of something real. Our moral code should celebrate that—our messy, unpredictable, glorious humanity." His post, resonating with thousands, marked a turning point in the digital dialogue—a shift from despair and cynicism toward a hopeful, transformative vision of ethics.

As dusk descended once more, the public forum of Moral Reclamation reconvened with renewed energy. Helena took the stage again, her voice now carrying the steady cadence of a revolutionary leader who had witnessed both the depths of despair and the heights of hope. "We are at a crossroads," she proclaimed, her tone resonant with passion, "and it is up to us to decide the legacy we leave behind. The old moral code served its purpose in a world that no longer exists. Now, we have the opportunity—and the responsibility—to write a new code, one that reflects our shared struggles, our diverse experiences, and our unyielding belief in the power of redemption." Her words, delivered with a blend of emotion and conviction, electrified the crowd. In that moment, the dialogue shifted from criticism to creation—a call to action that was both revolutionary and deeply personal.

In the aftermath of Helena's speech, as the crowd dispersed into the cool night, there was a tangible sense that something profound had begun. The process of rewriting the moral code was no longer a distant dream, but an active, collaborative endeavour—a movement that was gaining momentum with every shared story and every small act of courage. For the first time in a long while, the people of Luminex felt that their voices—fragile, imperfect, and fiercely true—could come together to build a future that was not dictated by fear or conformity, but by the boundless potential of authentic connection.

In that quiet, transformative twilight, the revolution was no longer solely about tearing down the old order. It had become about creating a new framework—one that acknowledged the pain of the past, honoured the sacrifices made, and celebrated the unpredictable, beautiful spectrum of human life. The rebels and citizens alike were ready to embrace the challenge, to join hands in a collective act of moral rebirth, and to rise together as architects of a future where every imperfection was a testament to the resilience of the human spirit.

And so, as the final embers of the day faded into the promise of a new dawn, the call to "Recode Luminex" resonated like a beacon. The movement had moved from dark, biting critique to a vibrant, revolutionary aspiration—a vision that, despite the price paid, held the promise of a world reborn through compassion, creativity, and an unwavering commitment to truth. In that stirring convergence of vice and virtue, every soul in Luminex was invited to contribute to a moral code that was as dynamic and evolving as life itself—a code that celebrated not perfection, but the brave, beautiful act of being human.

CHAPTER TEN

Dawn of a New Ethos

The night before the new dawn, Luminex lay quiet in a way that felt almost sacred—a city battered by conflict and sacrifice, yet ready, somehow, for rebirth. The echoes of past struggles still resonated in every cracked pavement and defiant mural, but beneath that residue of hardship, there was an unmistakable stirring of hope. It was as if the scars of revolution had begun to form a map, guiding the citizens toward a future where the old burdens of rigidity would be replaced by a liberating embrace of what it truly meant to be human.

In a long-abandoned building that had once served as a forgotten archive of the city's bureaucratic past, a small group of visionaries gathered. They were a mix of old rebels and fresh faces—those who had fought tooth and nail for change, and those who were only just beginning to understand its profound possibility. Here, among yellowed documents and the soft hum of a restored generator, the group set about planning what they called "The New Ethos Initiative."

Lena, whose journey had spanned from fierce rebellion to deep introspection, led the discussion with a quiet yet resolute determination. "We've paid a heavy price for our freedom," she began, her eyes soft but unyielding, "and while we must honour the sacrifices that brought us here, it is time to envision what comes next. The old moral codes, the rigid structures that once confined us—they have crumbled. Now, we have the rare opportunity to rebuild from the ground up, to create an ethos that reflects the full spectrum of our humanity: our defiance and our compassion, our chaos and our creativity."

Her words hung in the air, imbued with both the memory of past hardships and a dawning certainty that a better way was within reach. Around her, the gathered group—artists, former activists, community organisers, and even a few reformed former enforcers—nodded, their expressions reflecting a shared yearning for transformation. They had all lived the bitter, painful lessons of rebellion; now they sought to channel that experience into something constructive—a new moral framework that was as inclusive as it was inspiring.

Victor, whose acerbic wit had once been a weapon of critique but had softened into a tool for reflection, took a moment to speak. "For years, we mocked the so-called 'ideal' morality that demanded perfection at every turn," he said, his voice now carrying a gentle cadence. "We revealed in the chaos of vice, and in doing so, we discovered that our greatest strengths often lay hidden in our flaws. It's time to stop seeing our scars as mere wounds—instead, let's view them as the intricate calligraphy of our life stories, proof of battles fought and lessons learned. Our new code must celebrate that, honour the raw, unfiltered truth of our journey."

The conversation moved slowly, as if each word was being weighed against the collective memory of loss and triumph. Helena, the former ethics professor whose lectures had once been laced with biting sarcasm and now resonated with visionary hope, added, "True progress is not about erasing our past, but about transforming it into a foundation for a better future. Our legacy—every heartbreak, every victory—must be woven into the very fabric of our new ethos. We are not starting from scratch; we are evolving. Our moral code must be flexible enough to grow with us, to accommodate our dreams, our failures, and our ever-changing realities."

Outside, the city began to stir as the first light of dawn crept over the horizon. The harsh neon lights that had once illuminated the chaotic nights of rebellion were now softening into a gentle glow that hinted at renewal. In a narrow street near The Crucible—a former warehouse turned sanctuary of creativity—residents emerged from their homes with cautious optimism. Some glanced at the freshly painted murals that declared messages of hope and unity, while others simply took a moment to breathe in the cool, crisp air, as if savouring the taste of possibility.

Digital screens in coffee shops and on public transit now displayed messages of a new beginning. One such screen showed a looping video montage: clips of protestors turned community volunteers, flash mobs evolving into organised street festivals, and quiet interviews with citizens sharing personal stories of transformation. The caption, in bold, hopeful letters, read: "Dawn of a New Ethos: Embrace the Full Spectrum of You." The visual was a stark contrast to the grim images of past strife—it was a promise that despite all that had been lost, something beautiful and resilient was emerging.

At The Crucible, the cultural epicentre of the revolution, preparations were underway for the first public "Dawn Assembly"—a city-wide event meant to mark the official birth of the New Ethos. In the sprawling space, converted into a temporary forum for dialogue and art, murals and digital projections intertwined. One side of the room displayed a giant mosaic of photographs capturing the raw moments of past protests and acts of defiance; the other side was lined with screens streaming messages from across Luminex, each one a personal testament to the journey from darkness to light. The atmosphere was electric, yet tempered by a palpable sense of collective healing. It was a space where the anger and pain of previous years had slowly begun to yield to a cautiously emerging hope—a hope that was as vibrant as it was vulnerable.

As the hours passed and the assembly drew nearer, a sense of unity settled over the rebels and citizens alike. In private conversations, people spoke not only of what they had lost but also of the small, yet profound, joys they had discovered along the way. A young woman recounted how she had found solace in writing poetry about her struggles, and how those words had become a lifeline for others. An elderly man spoke of rediscovering long-forgotten passions—music, art, even simple acts of kindness—that had once been buried beneath layers of routine and resignation. These stories, shared in hushed tones and earnest exchanges, were the building blocks of the New Ethos—a collective narrative that recognised that progress was not a linear march toward a predetermined goal, but a tapestry woven from every thread of human experience.

In the meeting room of the community centre, the visionaries began drafting the preliminary outline of what would become the New Ethos Manifesto. The document was intended to be a living, evolving guide—a set of principles that would not only honour the past but also inspire future generations to embrace change with courage and compassion. "We must build a code that is as dynamic as life itself," Victor wrote on a whiteboard, his handwriting bold and determined. "One that allows for contradictions, that values empathy as much as audacity, that recognises the inherent worth in every individual, no matter how flawed." His declaration was met with quiet, resolute applause, as each participant felt the stirring of something profound—a realisation that for the first time in years, they had a hand in shaping not just their destiny, but the moral future of their entire city.

As the dawn Assembly approached, Helena invited everyone present to take a moment of collective reflection. "Tonight, we stand on the brink of a new era," she said, her voice soft but unwavering. "Our journey has been long and fraught with sacrifice, but we have also learned that true transformation comes not from denying our past, but from embracing it fully—its pain, its beauty, its complexity. We have redefined what it means to be rebellious, to be authentic, and now we have the opportunity to rewrite the rules that govern our lives. Let our New Ethos be a beacon—a living testament that the human spirit is capable of remarkable growth when we dare to be all that we are."

In that moment, as the early morning light spilled over the city and the assembly prepared to step into the public square, a collective sense of purpose permeated the air. The rebels, once driven by anger and defiance, now carried within them a quiet, revolutionary hope—a belief that the future was not predetermined by the failures of the past, but could be remade by the shared vision of a community united in its diversity.

With hearts full and spirits unburdened by the weight of old expectations, they emerged from the community centre into a city that was, at last, beginning to awaken. The air was cool and crisp, filled with the promise of new beginnings. On every corner, whispers of the New Ethos grew louder—a call for every citizen to embrace their true selves, to live with compassion, creativity, and unyielding authenticity. And as the first rays of dawn broke over Luminex, painting the sky with hues of gold and rose, it became clear that a transformation was underway—a metamorphosis not just of buildings or systems, but of hearts and minds.

In that gentle, hopeful light, the people of Luminex took their first tentative steps toward a future defined by possibility rather than fear—a future where the old moral code was not merely dismantled, but replaced by something richer, more inclusive, and more true to the diverse tapestry of human experience. It was the dawn of a new ethos—a revolution of the spirit, where every individual had a voice, and every voice, in turn, helped to shape a world where progress was measured not by the absence of struggle, but by the courage to transform that struggle into a foundation for lasting, meaningful change.

As the first light of dawn gave way to the full glow of morning, Luminex began to reveal its new face. The city's once-cracked facades now shimmered under a gentle sun, and the harsh neon of the rebel nights softened into warm hues of gold and amber. It was in this transitional time, when darkness and light converged, that the people of Luminex started to feel the stirrings of a profound metamorphosis—a reawakening of spirit that promised to reshape not only their physical world but also the very values that had once confined them.

Across neighbourhoods that had borne the scars of revolt, citizens emerged to greet the day with tentative smiles and a quiet, collective determination. In the vibrant park where community gardens now flourished, neighbours worked side by side—planting, tending, and laughing together as if each seed they sowed was a promise for the future. The air, filled with the sweet scent of fresh earth and the sound of gentle conversation, felt like a silent celebration of life reborn. In this reclaimed space, every small act of nurturing was seen as a defiant stand against the old order—a declaration that the future would be built on compassion as much as on creativity.

At a newly established community hub—a repurposed cultural centre that had once been a symbol of the city's bureaucratic past—the first "Dawn Assembly" was taking shape. The room, brightened by natural light streaming through large windows, buzzed with the energy of people eager to share their visions for the future. Artists, activists, teachers, and reformed officials gathered around circular tables, their discussions now brimming with ideas that promised a new moral landscape. The conversations, once heavy with the grief of sacrifice, had evolved into creative brainstorming sessions. Here, they debated not only what should be discarded from the old moral code but also what noble values might be resurrected and reinterpreted to suit their current reality.

Lena, who had guided the movement through its darkest hours, now stood before a projection screen in the center of the assembly. Her tone was no longer cautious or tinged with the pain of past losses—it was clear, passionate, and forward-looking. "We have witnessed the high cost of progress," she began, her eyes scanning the hopeful faces before her, "but that cost has given us wisdom, resilience, and an unbreakable bond with one another. Today, we choose not to dwell solely on what we've lost but to embrace what we can build together. Our new ethos will be a living testament to our journey—a code that honours our struggles and transforms them into the principles that will guide us into a brighter future."

A murmur of agreement rippled through the room. Helena, her voice gentle yet resonant, stepped forward next. “For too long, morality was dictated from above—a rigid framework that left little room for the messiness of life. Now, we have the chance to reclaim our moral compass from within. We are the architects of our destiny. Let us not be defined by the fears of yesterday, but by the promise of what we can achieve tomorrow.” Her words, echoing with both the wisdom of experience and the excitement of possibility, inspired a wave of applause that filled the hub with renewed energy.

Outside the assembly, the impact of this collective vision was beginning to manifest on the city’s streets. In a busy plaza once dominated by the cold glare of corporate billboards, a giant mural now rose—a living artwork depicting a tree whose branches reached upward, interwoven with images of people from all walks of life. The tree, painted in hues of vibrant green and soft pastel, symbolized growth and renewal. Its roots, visible and raw, spoke of history and sacrifice, yet its flourishing canopy promised an abundant future. Below the tree, in elegant, flowing script, the words “Our Future Grows from Our Truth” served as a rallying cry for a city eager to redefine itself.

Digital platforms, too, buzzed with the energy of this new beginning. The underground forum that had once been the battleground of raw dissent now had a new thread: “Dawn of a New Ethos.” Here, users from across Luminex posted not only critiques of the old order but also sketches of ideas for a future built on shared values—stories of transformation, collaborative art projects, and even blueprints for community-driven policies. One post, featuring a mosaic of photographs that spanned generations, was captioned, “Together, We Rebuild.” The post quickly amassed hundreds of likes and heartfelt comments, as people found solace and inspiration in the possibility of unity through a reimagined moral code.

A group of local innovators had taken the idea further by launching an online platform that served as a digital town hall.

Dubbed "The Heart of Luminex," the platform allowed citizens to propose, debate, and vote on various community projects and ethical guidelines. What began as a small, experimental forum rapidly evolved into a powerful tool for democratic participation—a virtual space where every voice could contribute to shaping the moral future of the city. In this new digital arena, the old hierarchies began to crumble as people from all walks of life found common ground. A post that read, "Our Morality Is Our Own," became a trending mantra, encapsulating the spirit of a community that was no longer content to have its values dictated by distant authorities.

As the day advanced, the energy in Luminex grew increasingly palpable. Public spaces that had once been battlegrounds of protest were now venues for cultural festivals and creative collaborations. In one such festival, held in the open courtyard of a refurbished museum, families, artists, and activists came together to celebrate their shared heritage and the promise of a renewed community. Traditional music mingled with modern beats, local cuisine was shared freely, and the air was filled with laughter—a sound that, in its simplicity, signified the triumph of human connection over enforced uniformity.

Amid these uplifting scenes, personal narratives of transformation continued to emerge. Daniel, the once strict schoolteacher whose outlook had been rigidly shaped by conventional morality, now led a community class on emotional literacy. His once-dogmatic lessons had given way to discussions about empathy, resilience, and the importance of embracing one's vulnerabilities. "It is in our willingness to confront our own imperfections that we find the courage to be truly human," he explained to a room full of attentive students. His transformation, a microcosm of the city's broader evolution, underscored the message that the future was not a destination defined by perfection, but a journey enriched by every experience—both the joyous and the painful.

Victor, whose earlier critiques of the old order had been sharp and cutting, now used his once-sardonic pen to write essays that celebrated the possibilities of the New Ethos. In one widely read piece, he reflected on the paradox of rebellion: "We once believed that tearing down the walls of conformity was the ultimate act of liberation. But true liberation, I have come to understand, lies in the art of rebuilding—to construct a future where our imperfections are not liabilities, but the very elements that make us extraordinary." His words resonated deeply, bridging the gap between the raw defiance of the past and the hopeful vision of the present.

The transformation was not merely ideological—it was profoundly tangible. In neighbourhoods that had long been mired in the dull routine of conformity, residents began organising spontaneous events that celebrated diversity and creativity. In a small town square, a mural competition was held where participants were invited to depict what "authenticity" meant to them. The resulting artworks were a riot of colours, symbols, and personal stories—each one a defiant declaration that the old, monochrome narrative was no longer acceptable. These public expressions of creativity were a living embodiment of the New Ethos, a visual and emotional statement that Luminex was ready to embrace the fullness of its humanity.

As the sun began to set on a day that had been filled with both introspection and inspiration, the leaders of the movement gathered once more at the community hub. They reviewed the feedback from the public workshops, the digital contributions that had poured in, and the heartfelt testimonies from those who had participated in "The Heart of Luminex." There was a sense of cautious optimism—a belief that the seeds of a new moral code were beginning to take root in the hearts of the citizens. Lena, addressing the group, said with a hopeful smile, "We are witnessing the birth of a collective conscience. It's not perfect yet, but every conversation, every shared idea, is a building block for something greater. We have the chance to create a moral code that is dynamic, compassionate, and rooted in our lived experiences."

Helena added, "This new morality will not be handed down from above; it will be crafted by us, through dialogue, through art, through every act of kindness and every moment of honest reflection. It is the promise that from our struggles, a richer, more inclusive future can emerge—a future where the price of progress is honoured not as a burden, but as the foundation of our shared triumph."

The discussion in the hub grew animated as plans were laid for the next phase of public engagement. They envisioned a series of city-wide festivals, art installations, and digital campaigns aimed at disseminating the core principles of the New Ethos. Every event would serve as a reminder that morality was not a fixed set of rules, but a living, evolving dialogue—a collective effort to redefine what it meant to live with authenticity, empathy, and creativity.

As the evening deepened, the atmosphere outside the community hub was charged with the promise of a new era. On the streets, lights began to twinkle with a gentle, inviting glow, and the cool night air carried whispers of possibility. In the midst of this unfolding transformation, the people of Luminex—no longer content to be mere subjects of a repressive moral code—had begun to write their own narrative, one that embraced the full spectrum of human experience.

And so, as the city settled into the quiet, reflective hours before midnight, a powerful realisation took hold: that in the synthesis of rebellious vice and reimagined virtue lay the key to a future unburdened by the old ways. The New Ethos was not simply a reaction against the past; it was a forward-looking, revolutionary blueprint for living—a testament to the enduring capacity of the human spirit to innovate, to heal, and to dream.

In that visionary twilight, every individual, every community, every digital voice in Luminex contributed to a grand mosaic of hope—a tapestry woven from the threads of shared struggle, triumph, and the unyielding belief that together, they could rewrite the very definition of what it meant to be moral. The seeds planted today would blossom into a legacy of compassion, resilience, and boundless creativity—a legacy that promised not only to honour the price of progress but to transform it into the currency of a truly liberated future.

As the first full light of day broke over Luminex, the city no longer appeared as a battleground of scars and memories, but as a vast canvas on the verge of renewal. The streets, softened by the gentle glow of morning, whispered of new beginnings. Every cracked pavement and every defaced wall now told stories of resilience, each remnant of the past transmuted into a foundation upon which the future would be built. The revolution, once marked by pain and sacrifice, had matured into something far more profound—a collective awakening that promised not only change, but the birth of an entirely new ethos.

In the heart of the city, where The Crucible had once roared with the cries of defiance, a new public space had emerged. It was a repurposed civic centre, its walls freshly painted with murals that combined bold, expressive strokes with intricate designs hinting at classical beauty. Here, people of all ages and walks of life gathered, drawn by the irresistible pull of hope. The air buzzed with anticipation as citizens prepared to celebrate "The New Dawn Festival," an event heralding the official launch of the New Ethos Manifesto—a living document that encapsulated the collective aspirations and hard-won wisdom of a community reborn.

On the expansive stage set up in the central plaza, Lena stepped forward. Her once battle-hardened features now shone with a quiet inner light. Standing before a sea of expectant faces, she spoke with a clarity that resonated like a clarion call. "Today," she began, her voice steady and filled with a visionary warmth, "we stand at the threshold of a future that we have built together. For years, we have fought for freedom, for authenticity, and for the right to define our own morality. Now, the dawn of a new ethos is upon us—a morality that embraces every facet of our being, that celebrates our imperfections, and that transforms our struggles into the very building blocks of a brighter tomorrow."

Her words were met with a swell of applause and murmurs of affirmation, as if each listener felt the stirring of a deep, collective transformation. Around her, the crowd was a living tapestry of diverse expression: old friends reunited after long separations, families who had once hidden behind the curtains of fear now emerging into the light, and even former adversaries—those who had once clashed in the heat of rebellion—sharing quiet smiles of reconciliation. It was as if the very act of gathering in this open space had healed old wounds, knitting together a fractured past into a hopeful vision for the future.

As Lena's speech gave way to a series of musical performances and poetic recitations, the festival evolved into a dynamic celebration of human creativity. The stage was alive with art and passion—an orchestra of voices that sang of loss transformed into love, of the darkness that had once held them captive now giving way to the light of possibility. A young violinist, her eyes glistening with the raw emotion of her music, played a haunting melody that seemed to capture the entire spectrum of the human spirit—from sorrow to joy, from despair to hope. Each note carried the promise of renewal, a reminder that even the most painful experiences could yield seeds of beauty.

In a nearby pavilion, community workshops unfolded. Citizens gathered in small groups to discuss the principles of the New Ethos Manifesto. Facilitators—people who had once been reluctant participants in the rebellion—now guided conversations with a blend of empathy and fervour. Topics ranged from the importance of embracing vulnerability to the need for a morality that could evolve in an ever-changing world. One elderly woman, her hands trembling yet determined, recounted how, for decades, she had lived by a strict moral code that left little room for error. "I spent my life fearing that one misstep would make me unworthy," she said softly. "But now, I see that every mistake, every scar, tells a story of survival and growth. Our new code will honour that. It will teach us that we are beautiful precisely because we are flawed."

The discussions rippled out into the digital realm as well. The underground platform—once a cauldron of raw, unsanitised truth—had blossomed into a hub of collaborative creation. Users from all corners of Luminex shared drafts of their ideas, debated the nuances of the new moral code, and contributed art, music, and literature that celebrated the full spectrum of their experiences. A series of livestreams under the hashtag #NewEthosNow attracted thousands of viewers, uniting people through their shared vision of a society where morality was not an oppressive mandate but a dynamic, inclusive dialogue.

In one of these streams, a young man whose transformation from corporate stoicism to creative passion had been nothing short of dramatic, spoke directly to the digital audience. "For so long, I measured my worth by the rigid standards imposed upon me," he said, his voice steady with newfound confidence. "But now, I understand that true virtue is not about perfection—it's about authenticity. It's about daring to be yourself, even when the world tells you that you're too messy, too unpredictable. Our future will be defined by our courage to embrace every part of who we are, and that is something no one can take away from us."

As the day wore on, the festival became a mosaic of interwoven experiences—each performance, each conversation, each quiet moment of reflection was a brushstroke in a grand, evolving portrait of the city. The visual arts installations, spread throughout public spaces, showcased works that merged traditional symbolism with modern rebel motifs. A massive sculpture in the central plaza, crafted from reclaimed materials and illuminated by soft, ambient light, depicted a human figure with outstretched arms, as if reaching for a future beyond the confines of the past. At its base, a plaque read, "In unity, we find our true strength. In our diversity, we discover the endless possibilities of our shared humanity."

As dusk approached once again, the collective spirit of the New Ethos seemed to infuse every corner of Luminex. The reverberations of the festival reached even the most unlikely places. In the corridors of corporate offices, employees who had once been the model of conformity began to exchange knowing glances—subtle signals that they, too, were beginning to question the sterile norms that had long defined their lives. In government districts, hushed conversations hinted at a growing awareness that the old ways were crumbling, not out of weakness, but because the people were choosing a more compassionate, inclusive path forward.

At the heart of the festival, as the day drew to a close and the warm hues of sunset bathed the city in a gentle glow, Helena returned to the stage for one final address. Her eyes, reflecting the myriad lights of a transformed city, shone with an inspiring clarity. "Today, we have taken the first bold steps toward a future where morality is not a chain that binds us, but a compass that guides us—one that is crafted by our own hands and hearts," she proclaimed. "The dawn of a new ethos is upon us—a testament to our resilience, our creativity, and our unyielding belief in the possibility of a better world. We stand here not as fragments of a broken past, but as the architects of a whole, vibrant future. Let our shared truth be the foundation upon which we build a society that honours every voice, every struggle, and every hope." Her words, delivered with a visionary passion that transcended the pain of past conflicts, stirred the crowd into a roar of approval—a sound that seemed to echo into the future.

In that transcendent moment, as the sun sank below the horizon and the sky burst into brilliant shades of orange and pink, every individual present felt the pulse of a new beginning. The New Ethos was not a distant ideal—it was a living, breathing reality, unfolding in every act of kindness, every creative spark, every shared moment of vulnerability. The revolution had not ended with the dismantling of the old moral code; it had evolved into a movement of renewal—a commitment to a future where every person could live freely, authentically, and with the full richness of their human experience.

As the festival came to a close and the crowds slowly dispersed into the welcoming arms of the night, the promise of a transformed Luminex lingered in the air like a gentle refrain. The city, once defined by stark divisions and oppressive rules, now hummed with the vibrant, hopeful notes of a collective vision—one that celebrated not only the triumphs of rebellion but also the quiet, enduring beauty of human connection.

And so, in the lingering twilight, as the first stars began to twinkle above a city reborn, the people of Luminex embraced the dawning of a new era—a time when the old shackles were replaced by the limitless potential of a morality reimagined. In every heartfelt smile, every whispered promise, and every defiant step forward, they affirmed their commitment to a future where truth was not confined by outdated dogmas, but liberated by the courage to redefine what it meant to be moral.

The dawn of this new ethos was not the end of the struggle—it was the beginning of a lifelong journey, a perpetual evolution of values and vision. With each new day, as Luminex awoke to the gentle promise of possibility, its citizens carried the legacy of their past sacrifices as a torch to light the way forward. They knew that challenges would arise, that there would be setbacks and moments of doubt, but they also knew that every moment of authentic living was a victory—a step closer to a world where morality was as dynamic, inclusive, and boundless as the human spirit itself.

Epilogue: The Endless Dance Of Virtue And Vice

In the quiet after the revolution, when the fervour of defiance had ebbed into a reflective stillness, Luminex revealed itself as a living testament to the paradox that had driven its transformation—a city where the endless dance of virtue and vice played out in every heartbeat, every whispered promise, every defiant smile. The struggle was far from over; it had only evolved into a dynamic, ceaseless interplay between opposing forces, each essential to the unfolding story of progress.

For centuries, morality in Luminex had been cast in rigid black and white—an unforgiving framework that dictated who was worthy and who was not. The old moral code, with its sterile prescriptions and punitive measures, had tried to snuff out the very human impulses that made life vibrant. Yet, in its suppression, it had unwittingly sown the seeds of rebellion. In tearing down those walls, the people discovered that what had once been denounced as vice was inseparable from virtue—the risk, the passion, the unpredictability that fueled creativity and the capacity for empathy. And so, in the aftermath of the uprising, the citizens of Luminex came to see that the journey toward true freedom was not a linear march toward absolute goodness, but rather an endless, intricate dance.

Walking through the transformed streets, one could no longer tell where virtue ended and vice began. A mural on a building's facade might depict a gentle hand extended in compassion intermingled with splashes of wild, rebellious colour—a visual allegory for a society that had learned to celebrate its contradictions. In every act of protest, every tender moment of personal loss and collective healing, the city pulsed with the knowledge that both sides of the spectrum were indispensable. The pain of sacrifice and the bittersweet rewards of progress mingled like the colours of a sunset—each hue essential to the full brilliance of the whole.

At community centres and digital forums alike, conversations had shifted from a focus on what needed to be destroyed to what could be rebuilt from the ashes. The people, once defined by their stark oppositions, were now writing a new narrative where each person was allowed to be both flawed and noble, defiant and compassionate. In these spaces, the old binaries dissolved into a more expansive language—a moral vocabulary that recognised that vulnerability and rebellion, when embraced with honesty, could give rise to an ethics that was as flexible as it was enduring.

Leaders like Lena and Helena, who had once rallied the city with their fiery declarations, now spoke with a calm conviction born of hard-won experience. They taught that the true strength of a society lay not in its ability to enforce uniformity, but in its capacity to absorb, adapt, and ultimately celebrate the full complexity of human existence. "Our journey," Lena would say in quiet gatherings, "is the very proof that the price of progress, though steep, is also the seed of our renewal. Every scar we bear, every misstep we learn from, becomes a stroke in the grand canvas of our shared future."

In homes and on quiet street corners, families gathered to share stories of the past and dreams for the future. The elders, who had once clung to the comforting certainty of old ways, now spoke of a time when life was measured in moments of connection rather than in rigid adherence to tradition. Their narratives, tinged with regret yet filled with hope, wove together the threads of loss and renewal into a tapestry that illuminated a future of possibility. Children listened wide-eyed as their parents recounted the struggles that had paved the way for this new era—a time when morality was no longer imposed from above, but co-created from within the hearts of all who dared to live honestly.

In the digital world, the transformation was equally profound. The underground platforms, once wild battlefields of unfiltered passion and raw dissent, had matured into spaces of collaborative creativity. Here, every shared essay, every piece of digital art, and every candid video testimony added a verse to the evolving anthem of the city—a reminder that our truths, however painful, were the foundation of a better tomorrow. Hashtags like #EternalDance and #OurMoralMelody trended as people from every corner of Luminex, and even beyond, joined in an open dialogue about the endless interplay between our darkest impulses and our brightest ideals.

As the seasons turned and the city continued to evolve, the revolution began to settle into a rhythm—a steady, relentless dance between the forces of vice and virtue that defined the very fabric of Luminex. New laws and policies were crafted not by imposing a single, rigid standard, but by inviting the voices of all its citizens to participate in shaping a morality that was as diverse and ever-changing as the people themselves. Public institutions, once symbols of bureaucratic control, now served as open forums for debate and creativity, where every opinion was valued and every story contributed to the collective conscience.

The endless dance of virtue and vice had taught the people of Luminex a simple yet revolutionary truth: that progress is not achieved by erasing our flaws, but by integrating them into a fuller picture of who we are. Our vulnerabilities, once seen as weaknesses to be hidden away, became the very sources of our strength. Each act of rebellion, every moment of tender defiance, was a step toward a future where morality was not a tool of oppression but a beacon of inclusive possibility.

In the soft glow of twilight, as the city reflected on its tumultuous past and gazed forward with hopeful eyes, it became clear that Luminex had transformed into something more than a battleground—it had become a living, breathing symphony of human spirit. The scars on its streets, the whispered confessions in its digital corridors, and the vibrant murals that now decorated its once-gray walls all told the same story: that the cost of progress was high, but so too were the rewards. And in that delicate balance, there lay an invitation to all—to join in the endless, evolving dance of virtue and vice, to celebrate every imperfection as a note in the grand melody of life.

As night gave way to dawn, and as the first rays of sunlight bathed the city in a promise of renewal, the people of Luminex carried with them the legacy of their struggles and the luminous vision of a future reborn. The revolution had not ended with the shattering of old codes; it had ignited a continuous journey toward a new moral horizon—one where every voice, every tear, and every act of defiance was woven into the fabric of a community determined to redefine what it meant to live with purpose and passion.

In that new day's light, the dance continued—a graceful, endless interplay of shadow and brilliance, of vice and virtue, each step a reminder that to be human is to embrace all that we are. And so, the city marched onward, its people united in the quiet, steadfast hope that the moral code they were creating would not only honour their past but illuminate a future where every soul was free to shine in its raw, unfiltered beauty.

www.ingramcontent.com/pod-product-compliance
Lightning Source LLC
LaVergne TN
LVHW041217150826
845673LV00001B/433

9798897445288